May Fowler Mistry is a shy, retiring book monster who lives in a cave somewhere in India. In summers, she eats, sleeps and reads books. In winters, well, she does the same. She is gentle and friendly and responds well to offerings of good books. She enjoys picking out her favourite stories from these books and telling them to passing birds, foxes, hikers, lizards. Talking Cub persuaded her to pick out some exciting stories of magicians and wizards so that children everywhere could read them. If you liked these, you can write to Talking Cub at editorial@speakingtiger.com and the Cub will pass on the message to its BBMF (best book monster friend).

The MAGIC SHOP

Classic Stories of Magicians, Wizards and Spellmakers

Introduction by **Subhadra Sen Gupta**
Edited by **May Fowler Mistry**

An Imprint of Speaking Tiger Books

TALKING CUB
Published by Speaking Tiger Books LLP
4381/4 Ansari Road, Daryaganj,
New Delhi–110002, India

This edition published in paperback by Talking Cub in
Speaking Tiger Books 2020

Edition copyright © Speaking Tiger 2020
Introduction copyright © Subhadra Sen Gupta 2020
Translation copyright for 'The Story of Goopy the Singer and
Bagha the Drummer' © Tilottama Shome 2020

ISBN 978-93-89958-07-2
eISBN 978-81-944908-9-0

10 9 8 7 6 5 4 3 2 1

The moral rights of the authors have been asserted.

All rights reserved.
No part of this publication may be reproduced,
transmitted, or stored in a retrieval system, in any form or
by any means, electronic, mechanical, photocopying,
recording or otherwise, without the prior
permission of the publisher.

This book is sold subject to the condition that it shall not,
by way of trade or otherwise, be lent, resold, hired out,
or otherwise circulated, without the publisher's
prior consent, in any form of binding or cover
other than that in which it is published.

Contents

Introduction *Subhadra Sen Gupta*	7
The Story of the Four Little Children Who Went Round the World *Edward Lear*	11
A Toy Princess *Mary De Morgan*	29
The Magic Shop *H.G. Wells*	47
The Magic Fish-bone *Charles Dickens*	63
The Nursery Alice *Lewis Carroll*	79
Ozma and the Little Wizard *L. Frank Baum*	111

The Princess and the Hedge-pig   119
    E. Nesbit

The Story of Goopy the Singer and Bagha the Drummer   145
    Upendrakishore Ray Chowdhury

Notes on Authors   169

introduction

SUBHADRA SEN GUPTA

First try and remember the oddest, scariest, funniest, most impossible dream you have ever had...

Maybe it was about meeting a Chinese paper dragon that hates noodles and loves biryani topped with idlis...

Or you are lost in a building where there are hundreds and hundreds of pink and purple rooms and you can't get out...

Or you meet the king of ghosts who entertains you with a kathak dance wearing shiny shoes made of the scales of a fish...

That is where this bunch of stories of fantasy, magic and spells that you are about to read begin.

In our dreams.

So it is reasonable to say that all these famous writers—from Edward Lear of Britain to Upendrakishore Ray Chowdhury of India—who wrote these stories must have been having wonderfully weird and whacky dreams every night.

As you read stories like 'The Story of the Four Little Children Who Went Round the World' by Edward Lear and 'The Nursery Alice' by Lewis Carroll you'll discover that fantasy stories are a great way to travel to strange, mindbogglingly lunatic lands. For example, the four children voyage across the oceans to land on an island made of water. An island made of water? You'll ask. How can that be? That is so, so impossible. We all know that all islands are lands that are surrounded by the sea and they float on water. Then if an island is made of water then won't it vanish in a micro millisecond of time? And things get even more puzzling when Alice meets a rabbit with a pocket watch and a queen of hearts who looks like a playing card.

Ah, my friend, you forget, these are fantasy stories and you don't have to be logical or reasonable or even sensible at all!

So put on your pink, heart-shaped glitter glasses; slip on a funny, zebra-striped T-shirt; make yourself a tall, orangey, lemony or greenish drink and settle down to have some fun. The beast called Quangle Wangle, a strangely spooky shopkeeper, a magical drummer and a very bad singer have some wonderful stories to tell you.

Sometimes I think that real life is much too realistic and rather a dull and boring recreation. I mean, who can possibly like getting up at six in the morning in the dead of winter, crawl out of the quilt to get ready and then stand at the bus stop sleepy and shivering to go to school? Or coming home all bone tired, with the schoolbag stuffed with homework when all you want to do is chill with your friends over some pizza. Adults can be so cruel to children.

That is why I recommend reading books.

Life gets interesting when you read. Then you can imagine Alice's friend the Cheshire Cat joining you in the bus and telling you a really awful joke about white mice eating custard pudding. And immediately your eyes would pop open in surprise. Are you sure, dear Cheshire Cat, that it was custard pudding and not rosogollas? you'll ask. And the Cheshire Cat will just smile. Soon the sun will come out in the school playground and who will you see strolling along towards you playing a giant drum totally out of beat? It is the magical drummer Bagha Byne of course!

When you begin reading books you will discover that you get dreams even at daytime.

So I recommend you finish all the deadly dull and desperately, dubiously, dumb homework and then open this book and get lost in the adventures of Princess Ozma and the Wizard of Oz, chat with the little princess who forgot to smile, and meet two of the stupidest kings on earth. Life is sure to become fun again.

Then after you have finished this book I have a suggestion on what you should do next. Get a notebook with lots of empty, lined pages inside. This notebook could have a happy magenta cover or a solemn grey one and the pages could be sky blue or coriander green. (My notebook has a black-and-white tiger-striped cover and the inside pages are turmeric yellow.) Then select your favourite pencil, pen or crayon. (I am using a very, very,very small pencil the size of my thumb.) Now close your eyes tight and remember all your weird, whacky, scary, happy, weepy, moody dreams. Then you write them all down in a story. Not hard at all to do.

I can guarantee you one thing. You will have so much fun you'll never stop writing, like ever. Or reading, like never ever! Or dreaming, like often!

Spellbinding stories await you here, my friend. Turn the page, start reading and have fun!

the story of the four little children who went round the world

EDWARD LEAR

Once upon a time, a long while ago, there were four little people whose names were

VIOLET,   SLINGSBY,   GUY,   and LIONEL;

and they all thought they should like to see the world. So they bought a large boat to sail quite round the world by sea, and then they were to come back on the other side by land. The boat was painted blue with green spots, and the sail was yellow with red stripes: and, when they set off, they only took a small Cat to steer and look after the boat, besides an elderly Quangle-Wangle, who had to cook the dinner and make the tea; for which purposes they took a large kettle.

For the first ten days they sailed on beautifully, and found plenty to eat, as there were lots of fish, and they had only to take them out of the sea with a long spoon, when the Quangle-Wangle instantly cooked them. The Pussy-Cat was fed with the bones, with which she expressed herself pleased, on the whole: so that all the party were very happy.

During the daytime, Violet chiefly occupied herself in putting salt water into a churn while her three brothers churned it violently, in the hope that it would turn into butter, which it seldom if ever did. In the evening they all retired into the tea-kettle, where they all managed to sleep very comfortably, while Pussy and the Quangle-Wangle managed the boat.

After a time, they saw some land at a distance; and, when they came to it, they found it was an island made of water quite surrounded by earth. Besides that, it was bordered by evanescent isthmuses, with a great gulf-stream running about all over it; so that it was perfectly beautiful, and contained only a single tree, 503 feet high.

When they had landed, they walked about, but found, to their great surprise, that the island was quite full of veal-cutlets and chocolate-drops, and nothing else. So they all climbed up the single high tree to discover, if possible, if there were any people; but having remained on the top of the tree for a week, and not seeing anybody, they naturally concluded that there were no inhabitants.

Accordingly, when they came down, they loaded the boat with two thousand veal-cutlets and a million of chocolate-drops; and these afforded them sustenance for more than a month, during which time they pursued their voyage with the utmost delight and apathy.

After this they came to a shore where there were no less than sixty-five great red parrots

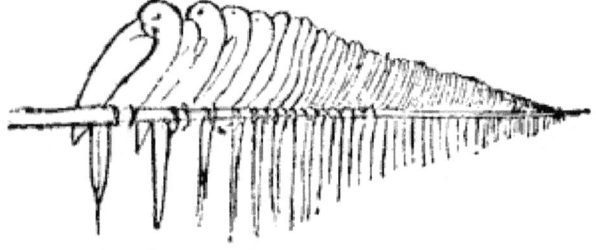

with blue tails, sitting on a rail all of a row, and all fast asleep. And I am sorry to say that the Pussy-Cat and the Quangle-Wangle crept softly, and bit off the tail-feathers of all the sixty-five parrots; for which Violet reproved them both severely.

Notwithstanding which, she proceeded to insert all the feathers—two hundred and sixty in number—in her bonnet; thereby causing it to have a lovely and glittering appearance, highly prepossessing and efficacious.

The next thing that happened to them was in a narrow part of the sea, which was so entirely full of fishes that the boat could go on no farther: so they remained there about six weeks, till they had eaten nearly all the fishes, which were soles, and all ready-cooked, and covered with shrimp-sauce, so that there was no trouble whatever.

And as the few fishes who remained uneaten complained of the cold, as well as of the difficulty they had in getting any sleep on account of the extreme noise made by the arctic bears and the tropical turnspits, which frequented the neighborhood in great numbers, Violet most amiably knitted a small woollen frock for several of the fishes, and Slingsby administered some opium-drops to them; through which kindness they became quite warm, and slept soundly.

Then they came to a country which was wholly covered with immense orange-trees of a vast size, and quite full of fruit. So they all landed, taking with them the tea-kettle, intending to gather some of the oranges, and place them in it. But, while they were busy about this, a most dreadfully high wind rose, and blew out most of the parrot-tail feathers from Violet's bonnet. That, however, was nothing compared with the calamity of the oranges falling down on their heads by millions and millions, which thumped and bumped and bumped and thumped them all so seriously, that they were obliged to run as hard as they could for their lives; besides that the sound of the oranges rattling on the tea-kettle was of the most fearful and amazing nature.

Nevertheless, they got safely to the boat, although considerably vexed and hurt; and the Quangle-Wangle's right foot was so knocked about, that he had to sit with his head in his slipper for at least a week.

This event made them all for a time rather melancholy: and perhaps they might never have become less so, had not Lionel, with a most praiseworthy devotion and perseverance, continued to stand on one leg, and whistle to them in a loud and lively manner; which diverted the whole party so extremely that they gradually recovered their spirits, and agreed that whenever they should reach home, they would subscribe towards a testimonial to Lionel, entirely made of gingerbread and raspberries, as an earnest token of their sincere and grateful infection.

After sailing on calmly for several more days, they came to another country, where they were much pleased and surprised to see a countless multitude of white mice with red eyes, all sitting in a great circle, slowly eating custard-pudding with the most satisfactory and polite demeanour.

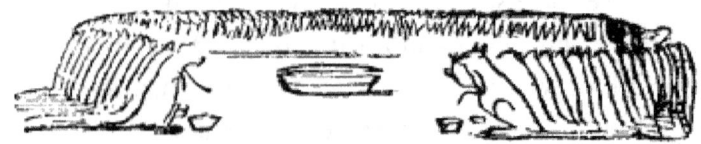

And as the four travellers were rather hungry, being tired of eating nothing but soles and oranges for so long a period, they held a council as to the propriety of asking the mice for some of their pudding in a humble and affecting manner, by which they could hardly be otherwise than gratified. It was agreed, therefore, that Guy should go and ask the mice, which he immediately did; and the result was, that they gave a walnut-shell only half full of custard diluted with water. Now, this displeased Guy, who said, 'Out of such a lot of pudding as you have got, I must say, you might have spared a somewhat larger quantity.' But no sooner had he finished speaking than the mice turned round at once, and sneezed at him in an appalling and vindictive manner (and it is impossible to imagine a more scroobious and unpleasant sound than that caused by the simultaneous sneezing of many millions of angry mice); so that Guy rushed back to the boat, having first shied his cap into the middle of the custard-pudding, by which means he completely spoiled the mice's dinner.

By and by the four children came to a country where there were no houses, but only an incredibly innumerable number of large bottles without corks, and of a dazzling and sweetly susceptible blue colour. Each of these blue bottles contained a Blue-Bottle-Fly; and all these interesting animals live continually together in the most copious and rural harmony: nor perhaps in many parts of the world is such perfect and abject happiness to be found. Violet and Slingsby and Guy and Lionel were greatly struck with this singular and instructive settlement and, having previously asked permission of the Blue-Bottle-Flies (which was most courteously granted), the boat was drawn up to the shore, and they proceeded to make tea in front of the bottles: but as they had no tea-leaves, they merely placed some pebbles in the hot water and the Quangle-Wangle played some tunes over it on an accordion, by which, of course, tea was made directly, and of the very best quality.

The four children then entered into conversation with the Blue-Bottle-Flies, who discoursed in a placid and genteel manner, though with a slightly buzzing accent, chiefly owing to the fact that they each held a small clothes-brush between their teeth, which naturally occasioned a fizzy, extraneous utterance.

'Why,' said Violet, 'would you kindly inform us, do you reside in bottles and, if in bottles at all, why not, rather, in green or purple, or, indeed, in yellow bottles?'

To which questions a very aged Blue-Bottle-Fly answered, 'We found the bottles here all ready to live in; that is to say, our great-great-great-great-great-grandfathers did, so we occupied them at once. And, when the winter comes on, we turn the bottles upside down, and consequently rarely feel the cold at all; and you know very well that this could not be the case with bottles of any other colour than blue.'

'Of course it could not,' said Slingsby. 'But, if we may take the liberty of inquiring, on what do you chiefly subsist?'

'Mainly on oyster-patties,' said the Blue-Bottle-Fly, 'and, when these are scarce, on raspberry vinegar and Russian leather boiled down to a jelly.'

'How delicious!' said Guy.

To which Lionel added, 'Huzz!' And all the Blue-Bottle-Flies said, 'Buzz!'

At this time, an elderly Fly said it was the hour for the evening-song to be sung and, on a signal being given, all the Blue-Bottle-Flies began to buzz at once in a sumptuous and sonorous manner, the melodious and mucilaginous sounds echoing all over the waters, and resounding across the tumultuous tops of the transitory titmice upon the intervening and verdant mountains with a serene and sickly suavity only known to the truly virtuous. The Moon was shining slobaciously from the star-bespangled sky, while her light irrigated the smooth and shiny sides and wings and backs of the Blue-Bottle-Flies with a peculiar and trivial splendour, while all Nature cheerfully responded to the cerulean and conspicuous circumstances.

In many long-after years, the four little travellers looked back to that evening as one of the happiest in all their lives; and it was already past midnight when—the sail of the boat having been set up by the Quangle-Wangle, the tea-kettle and churn placed in their respective positions, and the Pussy-Cat stationed at the helm—the children each took a last and affectionate farewell of the Blue-Bottle-Flies, who walked down in a body to the water's edge to see the travellers embark.

As a token of parting respect and esteem, Violet made a curtsey quite down to the ground, and stuck one of her few remaining parrot-tail feathers into the back hair of the most pleasing of the Blue-Bottle-Flies; while Slingsby, Guy, and Lionel offered them three small boxes, containing, respectively, black pins, dried figs and Epsom salts, and thus they left that happy shore forever.

Overcome by their feelings, the four little travellers instantly jumped into the tea-kettle, and fell fast asleep. But all along the shore, for many hours, there was distinctly heard a sound of severely-suppressed sobs, and of a vague multitude of living creatures using their pocket-handkerchiefs in a subdued simultaneous snuffle, lingering sadly along the walloping waves as the boat sailed farther and farther away from the Land of the Happy Blue-Bottle-Flies.

Nothing particular occurred for some days after these events, except that, as the travellers were passing a low tract of sand, they perceived an unusual and gratifying spectacle namely, a large number of Crabs and Crawfish—perhaps six or seven hundred—sitting by the water-side, and endeavouring to disentangle a vast heap of pale pink worsted, which they moistened at intervals with a fluid composed of lavender-water and white-wine negus.

'Can we be of any service to you, O crusty Crabbies?' said the four children.

'Thank you kindly,' said the Crabs consecutively. 'We are trying to make some worsted mittens, but do not know how.'

On which Violet, who was perfectly acquainted with the art of mitten-making, said to the Crabs, 'Do your claws unscrew, or are they fixtures?'

'They are all made to unscrew,' said the Crabs and

forthwith they deposited a great pile of claws close to the boat, with which Violet uncombed all the pale pink worsted, and then made the loveliest mittens with it you can imagine. These the Crabs, having resumed and screwed on their claws, placed cheerfully upon their wrists, and walked away rapidly on their hind-legs, warbling songs with a silvery voice and in a minor key.

After this, the four little people sailed on again till they came to a vast and wide plain of astonishing dimensions, on which nothing whatever could be discovered at first but, as the travellers walked onward, there appeared in the extreme and dim distance a single object, which on a nearer approach, and on an accurately cutaneous inspection, seemed to be somebody in a large white wig, sitting on an arm-chair made of sponge-cakes and oyster-shells. 'It does not quite look like a human being,' said Violet doubtfully nor could they make out what it really was, till the Quangle-Wangle (who had previously been round the world) exclaimed softly in a loud voice, 'It is the co-operative Cauliflower!'

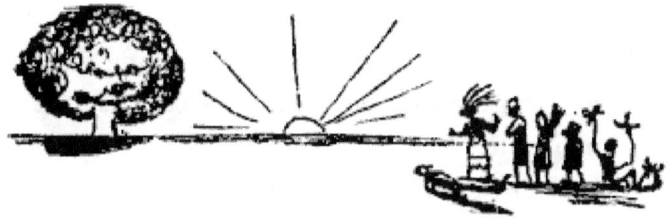

And so, in truth, it was: and they soon found that what they had taken for an immense wig was in reality the top of the Cauliflower; and that he had no feet at all, being able to walk tolerably well with a fluctuating and graceful movement on a single cabbage-stalk—an accomplishment which naturally saved him the expense of stockings and shoes.

Presently, while the whole party from the boat was gazing at him with mingled affection and disgust, he suddenly arose, and, in a somewhat plumdomphious manner, hurried off towards the setting sun—his steps supported by two superincumbent confidential Cucumbers, and a large number of Waterwagtails proceeding in advance of him by three and three in a row till he finally disappeared on the brink of the western sky in a crystal cloud of sudorific sand.

So remarkable a sight, of course, impressed the four children very deeply and they returned immediately to their boat with a strong sense of undeveloped asthma and a great appetite.

Shortly after this, the travellers were obliged to sail directly below some high overhanging rocks, from the top of one of which a particularly odious little boy, dressed in rose-coloured knickerbockers, and with a pewter plate upon his head, threw an enormous pumpkin at the boat, by which it was instantly upset.

But this upsetting was of no consequence, because all the party knew how to swim very well: and, in fact, they preferred swimming about till after the moon rose when, the water growing chilly, they sponge-taneously entered the boat. Meanwhile the Quangle-Wangle threw back the pumpkin with immense force, so that it hit the rocks where the malicious little boy in rose-coloured knickerbockers was sitting; when, being quite full of lucifer-matches, the pumpkin exploded surreptitiously into a thousand bits; whereon the rocks instantly took fire, and the odious little boy became unpleasantly hotter and hotter and hotter, till his knickerbockers were turned quite green, and his nose was burnt off.

Two or three days after this had happened, they came to another place, where they found nothing at all except some wide and deep pits full of mulberry-jam. This is the property of the tiny, yellow-nosed Apes who abound in these districts, and who store up the mulberry-jam for their food in winter, when they mix it with pellucid pale periwinkle-soup, and serve it out in wedgewood china-bowls, which grow freely all over that part of the country. Only one of the yellow-nosed Apes was on the spot, and he was fast asleep; yet the four travellers and the Quangle-Wangle and Pussy were so terrified by the violence and sanguinary sound of his snoring, that they merely took a small cupful of the jam, and returned to re-embark in their boat without delay.

What was their horror on seeing the boat (including the churn and the tea-kettle) in the mouth of an enormous Seeze Pyder, an aquatic and ferocious creature truly dreadful to behold, and, happily, only met with in those excessive longitudes! In a moment, the beautiful boat was bitten into fifty-five thousand million hundred billion bits; and it instantly became quite clear that Violet, Slingsby, Guy, and Lionel could no longer preliminate their voyage by sea.

The four travellers were therefore obliged to resolve on pursuing their wanderings by land: and, very fortunately, there happened to pass by at that moment an elderly Rhinoceros, on which they seized; and, all four mounting on his back—the Quangle-Wangle sitting on his horn, and holding on by his ears, and the Pussy-Cat swinging at the end of his tail—they set off, having only four small beans and three pounds of mashed potatoes to last through their whole journey.

They were, however, able to catch numbers of the chickens and turkeys and other birds who incessantly alighted on the head of the Rhinoceros for the purpose of gathering the seeds of the rhododendron-plants which grew there; and these creatures they cooked in the most translucent and satisfactory manner by means of a fire lighted on the end of the Rhinoceros's back. A crowd of Kangaroos and gigantic Cranes accompanied them, from feelings of curiosity and complacency; so that they were never at a loss for company, and went onward, as it were, in a sort of profuse and triumphant procession.

Thus in less than eighteen weeks they all arrived safely at home, where they were received by their admiring relatives with joy tempered with contempt, and where they finally resolved to carry out the rest of their travelling-plans at some more favourable opportunity.

As for the Rhinoceros, in token of their grateful adherence, they had him killed and stuffed directly, and then set him up outside the door of their father's house as a diaphanous doorscraper.

a toy princess

MARY DE MORGAN

More than a thousand years ago, in a country quite on the other side of the world, it fell out that the people all grew so very polite that they hardly ever spoke to each other. And they never said more than was quite necessary, as 'Just so,' 'Yes indeed,' 'Thank you,' and 'If you please'. And it was thought to be the rudest thing in the world for anyone to say they liked or disliked, or loved or hated, or were happy or miserable. No one ever laughed aloud, and if any one had been seen to cry they would at once have been avoided by their friends.

The king of this country married a princess from a neighbouring land, who was very good and beautiful, but the people in her own home were as unlike her husband's people as it was possible to be. They laughed, and talked, and were noisy and merry when they were happy, and cried and lamented if they were sad. In fact, whatever they felt they showed at once, and the princess was just like them.

So when she came to her new home, she could not at all understand her subjects, or make out why there was no shouting and cheering to welcome her, and why everyone was so distant and formal. After a time, when she found they never changed, but were always the same, just as stiff and quiet, she wept, and began to pine for her own old home.

Every day she grew thinner and paler. The courtiers were much too polite to notice how ill their young queen looked; but she knew it herself, and believed she was going to die.

Now she had a fairy godmother, named Taboret, whom she loved very dearly, and who was always kind to her. When she knew her end was drawing near she sent for her godmother, and when she came had a long talk with her quite alone.

No one knew what was said, and soon afterwards a little princess was born, and the queen died. Of course all the courtiers were sorry for the poor queen's death, but it would have been thought rude to say so. So, although there was a grand funeral, and the court put on mourning, everything else went on much as it had done before.

The little baby was christened Ursula, and given to some court ladies to be taken charge of. Poor little princess! She cried hard enough, and nothing could stop her.

All her ladies were frightened, and said that they had not heard such a dreadful noise for a long time. But, till she was about two years old, nothing could stop her crying when she was cold or hungry, or crowing when she was pleased.

After that she began to understand a little what was meant when her nurses told her, in cold, polite tones, that she was being naughty, and she grew much quieter.

She was a pretty little girl, with a round baby face and big merry blue eyes; but as she grew older, her eyes grew less and less merry and bright, and her fat little face grew thin and pale. She was not allowed to play with any other children, lest she might learn bad manners; and she was not taught any games or given any toys. So she passed most of her time, when she was not at her lessons, looking out of the window at the birds flying against the clear blue sky; and sometimes she would give a sad little sigh when her ladies were not listening.

One day the old fairy Taboret made herself invisible, and flew over to the king's palace to see how things were going on there. She went straight up to the nursery, where she found poor little Ursula sitting by the window, with her head leaning on her hand.

It was a very grand room, but there were no toys or dolls about, and when the fairy saw this, she frowned to herself and shook her head.

'Your Royal Highness's dinner is now ready,' said the head nurse to Ursula.

'I don't want any dinner,' said Ursula, without turning her head.

'I think I have told your Royal Highness before that it is not polite to say you don't want anything, or that you don't like it,' said the nurse. 'We are waiting for your Royal Highness.'

So the princess got up and went to the dinner-table, and Taboret watched them all the time. When she saw how pale little Ursula was, and how little she ate, and that there was no talking or laughing allowed, she sighed and frowned even more than before, and then she flew back to her fairy home, where she sat for some hours in deep thought.

At last she rose, and went out to pay a visit to the largest shop in Fairyland.

It was a queer sort of shop. It was neither a grocer's, nor a draper's, nor a hatter's. Yet it contained sugar, and dresses, and hats. But the sugar was magic sugar, which transformed any liquid into which it was put; the dresses each had some special charm, and the hats were wishing-caps. It was, in fact, a shop where every sort of spell or charm was sold.

Into this shop Taboret flew; and as she was well known there as a good customer, the master of the shop came forward to meet her at once, and bowing, begged to know what he could get for her.

'I want,' said Taboret, 'a princess.'

'A princess!' said the shopman, who was in reality an old wizard. 'What size do you want it? I have one or two in stock.'

'It must look now about six years old. But it must grow.'

'I can make you one,' said the wizard, 'but it'll come rather expensive.'

'I don't mind that,' said Taboret. 'See! I want it to look exactly like this,' and so saying she took a portrait of Ursula out of her bosom and gave it to the old man, who examined it carefully.

'I'll get it for you,' he said. 'When will you want it?'

'As soon as possible,' said Taboret. 'By tomorrow evening if possible. How much will it cost?'

'It'll come to a good deal,' said the wizard, thoughtfully. 'I have such difficulty in getting these things properly made in these days. What sort of voice is it to have?'

'It need not be at all talkative,' said Taboret, 'so that won't add much to the price. It need only say, "If you please," "No, thank you," "Certainly," and "Just so."'

'Well, under those circumstances,' said the wizard, 'I will do it for four cats' footfalls, two fish's screams, and two swans' songs.'

'It is too much,' cried Taboret. 'I'll give you the footfalls and the screams, but to ask for swans' songs!'

She did not really think it dear, but she always made a point of trying to beat tradesmen down.

'I can't do it for less,' said the wizard, 'and if you think it too much, you'd better try another shop.'

'As I am really in a hurry for it, and cannot spend time in searching about, I suppose I must have it,' said Taboret; 'but I consider the price very high. When will it be ready?'

'By tomorrow evening.'

'Very well, then, be sure it is ready for me by the time I call for it, and whatever you do, don't make it at all noisy or rough in its ways'; and Taboret swept out of the shop and returned to her home.

Next evening she returned and asked if her job was done.

'I will fetch it, and I am sure you will like it,' said the wizard, leaving the shop as he spoke.

Presently he came back, leading by the hand a pretty little girl of about six years—a little girl so like the Princess Ursula that no one could have told them apart.

'Well,' said Taboret, 'it looks well enough. But are you sure that it's a good piece of workmanship, and won't give way anywhere?'

'It's as good a piece of work as ever was done,' said the wizard, proudly, striking the child on the back as he spoke. 'Look at it! Examine it all over, and see if you find a flaw anywhere. There's not one fairy in twenty who could tell it from the real thing, and no mortal could.'

'It seems to be fairly made,' said Taboret, approvingly, as she turned the little girl round. 'Now I'll pay you, and then will be off'; with which she raised her wand in the air and waved it three times, and there arose a series of strange sounds. The first was a low tramping, the second shrill and piercing screams, the third voices of wonderful beauty, singing a very sorrowful song. The wizard caught all the sounds and pocketed them at once, and Taboret, without ceremony, picked up the child, took her head downwards under her arm, and flew away.

At court that night the little princess had been naughty, and had refused to go to bed. It was a long time before her ladies could get her into her crib, and when she was there, she did not really go to sleep, only lay still and pretended, till everyone went away; then she got up and stole noiselessly to the window, and sat down on the window-seat all curled up in a little bunch, while she looked out wistfully at the moon. She was such a pretty soft little thing, with all her warm bright hair falling over her shoulders, that it would have been hard for most people to be angry with her. She leaned her chin on her tiny white hands, and as she gazed out, the tears rose to her great blue eyes; but remembering that her ladies would call this naughty, she wiped them hastily away with her nightgown sleeve.

'Ah moon, pretty bright moon!' she said to herself, 'I wonder if they let you cry when you want to. I think I'd like to get up there and live with you; I'm sure it would be nicer than being here.'

'Would you like to go away with me?' said a voice close beside her; and looking up she saw a funny old woman in a red cloak, standing near to her. She was not frightened, for the old woman had a kind smile and bright black eyes, though her nose was hooked and her chin long.

'Where would you take me?' said the little princess, sucking her thumb, and staring with all her might.

'I'd take you to the sea-shore, where you'd be able to play about on the sands, and where you'd have some little boys and girls to play with, and no one to tell you not to make a noise.'

'I'll go,' cried Ursula, springing up at once.

'Come along,' said the old woman, taking her tenderly in her arms and folding her in her warm red cloak. Then they rose up in the air, and flew out of the window, right away over the tops of the houses.

The night air was sharp, and Ursula soon fell asleep; but still they kept flying on, on, over hill and dale, for miles and miles, away from the palace, towards the sea.

Far away from the court and the palace, in a tiny fishing village, on the sea, was a little hut where a fisherman named Mark lived with his wife and three children. He was a poor man, and lived on the fish he caught in his little boat. The children, Oliver, Philip, and little Bell, were rosy-cheeked and bright-eyed. They played all day long on the shore, and shouted till they were hoarse. To this village the fairy bore the still sleeping Ursula, and gently placed her on the doorstep of Mark's cottage; then she kissed her cheeks, and with one gust blew the door open, and disappeared before anyone could come to see who it was.

The fisherman and his wife were sitting quietly within. She was making the children clothes, and he was mending his net, when without any noise the door opened and the cold night air blew in.

'Wife,' said the fisherman, 'just see who's at the door.'

The wife got up and went to the door, and there lay Ursula, still sleeping soundly, in her little white nightdress.

The woman gave a little scream at sight of the child, and called to her husband.

'Husband, see, here's a little girl!' and so saying she lifted her in her arms, and carried her into the cottage. When she was brought into the warmth and light, Ursula awoke, and sitting up, stared about her in fright. She did not cry, as another child might have done, but she trembled very much, and was almost too frightened to speak.

Oddly enough, she had forgotten all about her strange flight through the air, and could remember nothing to tell the fisherman and his wife, but that she was the Princess Ursula; and, on hearing this, the good man and woman thought the poor little girl must be a trifle mad. However, when they examined her little nightdress, made of white fine linen and embroidery, with a crown worked in one corner, they agreed that she must belong to very grand people. They said it would be cruel to send the poor little thing away on such a cold night, and they must of course keep her till she was claimed. So the woman gave her some warm bread-and-milk, and put her to bed with their own little girl.

In the morning, when the court ladies came to wake Princess Ursula, they found her sleeping as usual in her little bed, and little did they think it was not she, but a toy Princess placed there in her stead. Indeed, the ladies were much pleased; for when they said 'It is time for your Royal Highness to arise,' she only answered, 'Certainly,' and let herself be dressed without another word. And as the time passed, and she was never naughty, and scarcely ever spoke, all said she was vastly improved, and she grew to be a great favourite.

The ladies all said that the young princess bid fair to have the most elegant manners in the country, and the king smiled and noticed her with pleasure.

In the meantime, in the fisherman's cottage far away, the real Ursula grew tall and straight as an alder and merry and light-hearted as a bird.

No one came to claim her, so the good fisherman and his wife kept her and brought her up among their own little ones. She played with them on the beach, and learned her lessons with them at school, and her old life had become like a dream she barely remembered.

But sometimes the mother would take out the little embroidered nightgown and show it to her, and wonder whence she came, and to whom she belonged.

'I don't care who I belong to,' said Ursula, 'they won't come and take me from you, and that's all I care about.' So she grew tall and fair, and as she grew, the toy princess, in her place at the court, grew too, and always was just like her, only that whereas Ursula's face was sunburnt and her cheeks red, the face of the toy princess was pale, with only a very slight tint in her cheeks.

Years passed, and Ursula at the cottage was a tall young woman, and Ursula at the court was thought to be the most beautiful there, and everyone admired her manners, though she never said anything but 'If you please,' 'No, thank you,' 'Certainly,' and 'Just so.'

The king was now an old man, and the fisherman Mark and his wife were grey-headed. Most of their fishing was now done by their eldest son, Oliver, who was their great pride. Ursula waited on them, and cleaned the house, and did the needlework, and was so useful that they could not have done without her. The fairy Taboret had come to the cottage from time to time, unseen by any one, to see Ursula, and always finding her healthy and merry, was pleased to think of how she had saved her from a dreadful life.

But one evening when she paid them a visit, not having been there for some time, she saw something which made her pause and consider. Oliver and Ursula were standing together watching the waves, and Taboret stopped to hear what they said—

'When we are married,' said Oliver, softly, 'we will live in that little cottage yonder, so that we can come and see them every day. But that will not be till little Bell is old enough to take your place, for how would my mother do without you?'

'And we had better not tell them,' said Ursula, 'that we mean to marry, or else the thought that they are preventing us will make them unhappy.'

When Taboret heard this she became grave, and pondered for a long time. At last she flew back to the court to see how things were going on there. She found the king in the middle of a state council. On seeing this, she at once made herself visible, when the king begged her to be seated near him, as he was always glad of her help and advice.

'You find us,' said His Majesty, 'just about to resign our sceptre into younger and more vigorous hands; in fact, we think we are growing too old to reign, and mean to abdicate in favour of our dear daughter, who will reign in our stead.'

'Before you do any such thing,' said Taboret, 'just let me have a little private conversation with you'; and she led the king into a corner, much to his surprise and alarm. In about half an hour he returned to the council, looking very white, and with a dreadful expression on his face, whilst he held a handkerchief to his eyes.

'My lords,' he faltered, 'pray pardon our apparently extraordinary behaviour. We have just received a dreadful blow; we hear on authority, which we cannot doubt, that our dear, dear daughter'—here sobs choked his voice, and he was almost unable to proceed—'is—is—in fact, not our daughter at all, and only a sham.'

Here the king sank back in his chair, overpowered with grief, and the fairy Taboret, stepping to the front, told the courtiers the whole story; how she had stolen the real princess, because she feared they were spoiling her, and how she had placed a toy princess in her place. The courtiers looked from one to another in surprise, but it was evident they did not believe her.

'The princess is a truly charming young lady,' said the prime minister.

'Has Your Majesty any reason to complain of her Royal Highness's conduct?' asked the old chancellor.

'None whatever,' sobbed the king, 'she was ever an excellent daughter.'

'Then I don't see,' said the chancellor, 'what reason

Your Majesty can have for paying any attention to what this—this person says.'

'If you don't believe me, you old idiots,' cried Taboret, 'call the princess here, and I'll soon prove my words.'

'By all means,' cried they.

So the king commanded that her Royal Highness should be summoned.

In a few minutes she came, attended by her ladies. She said nothing, but then she never did speak till she was spoken to. So she entered, and stood in the middle of the room silently.

'We have desired that your presence be requested,' the king was beginning, but Taboret without any ceremony advanced towards her, and struck her lightly on the head with her wand. In a moment the head rolled on the floor, leaving the body standing motionless as before, and showing that it was but an empty shell.

'Just so,' said the head, as it rolled towards the king, and he and the courtiers nearly swooned with fear.

When they were a little recovered, the king spoke again. 'The fairy tells me,' he said, 'that there is somewhere a real princess whom she wishes us to adopt as our daughter. And in the meantime let her Royal Highness be carefully placed in a cupboard, and a general mourning be proclaimed for this dire event.'

So saying he glanced tenderly at the body and head, and turned weeping away.

So it was settled that Taboret was to fetch Princess

Ursula, and the king and council were to be assembled to meet her.

That evening the fairy flew to Mark's cottage, and told them the whole truth about Ursula, and that they must part from her.

Loud were their lamentations, and great their grief, when they heard she must leave them. Poor Ursula herself sobbed bitterly.

'Never mind,' she cried after a time, 'if I am really a great princess, I will have you all to live with me. I am sure the king, my father, will wish it, when he hears how good you have all been to me.'

On the appointed day, Taboret came for Ursula in a grand coach and four, and drove her away to the court. It was a long, long drive; and she stopped on the way and had the princess dressed in a splendid white silk dress trimmed with gold, and put pearls round her neck and in her hair, that she might appear properly at court.

The king and all the council were assembled with great pomp, to greet their new princess, and all looked grave and anxious. At last the door opened, and Taboret appeared, leading the young girl by the hand.

'That is your father!' said she to Ursula, pointing to the king; and on this, Ursula, needing no other bidding, ran at once to him, and putting her arms round his neck, gave him a sounding kiss.

His Majesty almost swooned, and all the courtiers shut their eyes and shivered.

'This is really!' said one.

'This is truly!' said another.

'What have I done?' cried Ursula, looking from one to another, and seeing that something was wrong, but not knowing what. 'Have I kissed the wrong person?' on hearing which everyone groaned.

'Come now,' cried Taboret, 'if you don't like her, I shall take her away to those who do. I'll give you a week, and then I'll come back and see how you're treating her. She's a great deal too good for any of you.'

So saying she flew away on her wand, leaving Ursula to get on with her new friends as best she might, but Ursula could not get on with them at all, as she soon began to see.

If she spoke or moved they looked shocked, and at last she was so frightened and troubled by them that she burst into tears, at which they were more shocked still.

'This is indeed a change after our sweet princess,' said one lady to another.

'Yes, indeed,' was the answer, 'when one remembers how even after her head was struck off she behaved so beautifully, and only said, "Just so."'

And all the ladies disliked poor Ursula, and soon showed her their dislike. Before the end of the week, when Taboret was to return, she had grown quite thin and pale, and seemed afraid of speaking above a whisper.

'Why, what is wrong?' cried Taboret, when she returned and saw how much poor Ursula had changed. 'Don't you like being here? Aren't they kind to you?'

'Take me back, dear Taboret,' cried Ursula, weeping.

'Take me back to Oliver, and Philip, and Bell. As for these people, I hate them.'

And she wept again.

Taboret only smiled and patted her head, and then went into the king and courtiers.

'Now, how is it,' she cried, 'I find the Princess Ursula in tears? And I am sure you are making her unhappy. When you had that bit of wood-and-leather princess, you could behave well enough to it, but now that you have a real flesh-and-blood woman, you none of you care for her.'

'Our late dear daughter—' began the king, when the fairy interrupted him.

'I do believe,' she said, 'that you would like to have the doll back again. Now I will give you your choice. Which will you have—my Princess Ursula, the real one, or your Princess Ursula, the sham?'

The king sank back into his chair.

'I am not equal to this,' he said. 'Summon the council, and let them settle it by vote.'

So the council were summoned, and the fairy explained to them why they were wanted.

'Let both princesses be fetched,' she said, and the toy princess was brought in with care from her cupboard, and her head stood on the table beside her, and the real princess came in with her eyes still red from crying and her bosom heaving.

'I should think there could be no doubt which one we would prefer,' said the prime minister to the chancellor.

'Then vote,' said Taboret and they all voted, and every

vote was for the sham Ursula, and not one for the real one. Taboret only laughed.

'You are a pack of sillies and idiots,' she said, 'but you shall have what you want' and she picked up the head, and with a wave of her wand stuck it on to the body, and it moved round slowly and said, 'Certainly,' just in its old voice; and on hearing this, all the courtiers gave something as like a cheer as they thought polite, whilst the old king could not speak for joy.

'We will,' he cried, 'at once make our arrangements for abdicating and leaving the government in the hands of our dear daughter' and on hearing this, the courtiers all applauded again.

But Taboret laughed scornfully, and taking up the real Ursula in her arms, flew back with her to Mark's cottage.

In the evening the city was illuminated, and there were great rejoicings at the recovery of the princess, but Ursula remained in the cottage and married Oliver, and lived happily with him for the rest of her life.

the magic shop

H.G. WELLS

I had seen the Magic Shop from afar several times; I had passed it once or twice, a shop window of alluring little objects, magic balls, magic hens, wonderful cones, ventriloquist dolls, the material of the basket trick, packs of cards that LOOKED all right, and all that sort of thing, but never had I thought of going in until one day, almost without warning, Gip hauled me by my finger right up to the window, and so conducted himself that there was nothing for it but to take him in. I had not thought the place was there, to tell the truth—a modest-sized frontage in Regent Street, between the picture shop and the place where the chicks run about just out of patent incubators, but there it was sure enough. I had fancied it was down nearer the Circus, or round the corner in Oxford Street, or even in Holborn; always over the way and a little inaccessible it had been, with something of the mirage in its position; but here it was now quite indisputably, and the fat end of Gip's pointing finger made a noise upon the glass.

'If I was rich,' said Gip, dabbing a finger at the Disappearing Egg, 'I'd buy myself that. And that'—which was The Crying Baby, Very Human—'and that,' which was a mystery, and called, so a neat card asserted, 'Buy One and Astonish Your Friends.'

'Anything,' said Gip, 'will disappear under one of those cones. I have read about it in a book.

'And there, dadda, is the Vanishing Halfpenny—only they've put it this way up so's we can't see how it's done.'

Gip, dear boy, inherits his mother's breeding, and he did not propose to enter the shop or worry in any way; only, you know, quite unconsciously he lugged my finger doorward, and he made his interest clear.

'That,' he said, and pointed to the Magic Bottle.

'If you had that?' I said; at which promising inquiry he looked up with a sudden radiance.

'I could show it to Jessie,' he said, thoughtful as ever of others.

'It's less than a hundred days to your birthday, Gibbles,' I said, and laid my hand on the door-handle.

Gip made no answer, but his grip tightened on my finger, and so we came into the shop.

It was no common shop this; it was a magic shop, and all the prancing precedence Gip would have taken in the matter of mere toys was wanting. He left the burthen of the conversation to me.

It was a little, narrow shop, not very well lit, and the door-bell pinged again with a plaintive note as we closed it behind us. For a moment or so we were alone and could glance about us. There was a tiger in papier-mache on the glass case that covered the low counter—a grave, kind-eyed tiger that waggled his head in a methodical manner; there were several crystal spheres, a china hand holding magic cards, a stock of magic fish-bowls in various sizes, and an immodest magic hat that shamelessly displayed its springs. On the floor were magic mirrors; one to draw you out long and thin, one to swell your head and vanish your legs, and one to make you short and fat like a draught; and while we were laughing at these the shopman, as I suppose, came in.

At any rate, there he was behind the counter—a curious, sallow, dark man, with one ear larger than the other and a chin like the toe-cap of a boot.

'What can we have the pleasure?' he said, spreading his long, magic fingers on the glass case; and so with a start we were aware of him.

'I want,' I said, 'to buy my little boy a few simple tricks.'

'Legerdemain?' he asked. 'Mechanical? Domestic?'

'Anything amusing?' said I.

'Um!' said the shopman, and scratched his head for a moment as if thinking. Then, quite distinctly, he drew from his head a glass ball. 'Something in this way?' he said, and held it out.

The action was unexpected. I had seen the trick done at entertainments endless times before—it's part of the common stock of conjurers—but I had not expected it here.

'That's good,' I said, with a laugh.

'Isn't it?' said the shopman.

Gip stretched out his disengaged hand to take this object and found merely a blank palm.

'It's in your pocket,' said the shopman, and there it was!

'How much will that be?' I asked.

'We make no charge for glass balls,' said the shopman politely. 'We get them,'—he picked one out of his elbow as he spoke—'free.' He produced another from the back of his neck, and laid it beside its predecessor on the counter. Gip regarded his glass ball sagely, then directed a look of inquiry at the two on the counter, and finally brought his round-eyed scrutiny to the shopman, who smiled.

'You may have those too,' said the shopman, 'and, if you DON'T mind, one from my mouth. SO!'

Gip counselled me mutely for a moment, and then in a profound silence put away the four balls, resumed my reassuring finger, and nerved himself for the next event.

'We get all our smaller tricks in that way,' the shopman remarked.

I laughed in the manner of one who subscribes to a jest. 'Instead of going to the wholesale shop,' I said. 'Of course, it's cheaper.'

'In a way,' the shopman said. 'Though we pay in the end. But not so heavily—as people suppose.... Our larger tricks, and our daily provisions and all the other things we want, we get out of that hat... And you know, sir, if you'll excuse my saying it, there ISN'T a wholesale shop, not for Genuine Magic goods, sir. I don't know if you noticed our inscription—the Genuine Magic shop.' He drew a business-card from his cheek and handed it to me. 'Genuine,' he said, with his finger on the word, and added, 'There is absolutely no deception, sir.'

He seemed to be carrying out the joke pretty thoroughly, I thought.

He turned to Gip with a smile of remarkable affability. 'You, you know, are the Right Sort of Boy.'

I was surprised at his knowing that, because, in the interests of discipline, we keep it rather a secret even at home; but Gip received it in unflinching silence, keeping a steadfast eye on him.

'It's only the Right Sort of Boy gets through that doorway.'

And, as if by way of illustration, there came a rattling at the door, and a squeaking little voice could be faintly heard. 'Nyar! I WARN 'a go in there, dadda, I WARN 'a go in there. Ny-a-a-ah!' and then the accents of a down-trodden parent, urging consolations and propitiations. 'It's locked, Edward,' he said.

'But it isn't,' said I.

'It is, sir,' said the shopman, 'always—for that sort of child,' and as he spoke we had a glimpse of the other youngster, a little, white face, pallid from sweet-eating and over-sapid food, and distorted by evil passions, a ruthless little egotist, pawing at the enchanted pane. 'It's no good, sir,' said the shopman, as I moved, with my natural helpfulness, doorward, and presently the spoilt child was carried off howling.

'How do you manage that?' I said, breathing a little more freely.

'Magic!' said the shopman, with a careless wave of the hand, and behold! sparks of coloured fire flew out of his fingers and vanished into the shadows of the shop.

'You were saying,' he said, addressing himself to Gip, 'before you came in, that you would like one of our "Buy One and Astonish your Friends" boxes?'

Gip, after a gallant effort, said 'Yes.'

'It's in your pocket.'

And leaning over the counter—he really had an extraordinarily long body—this amazing person produced the article in the customary conjurer's manner. 'Paper,' he said, and took a sheet out of the empty hat with the springs; 'string,' and behold his mouth was a string-box, from which he drew an unending thread, which when he had tied his parcel he bit off—and, it seemed to me, swallowed the ball of string. And then he lit a candle at the nose of one of the ventriloquist's dummies, stuck one of his fingers (which had become sealing-wax red) into the flame, and so sealed the parcel. 'Then there was the Disappearing Egg,' he remarked, and produced one from within my coat-breast and packed it, and also The Crying Baby, Very Human. I handed each parcel to Gip as it was ready, and he clasped them to his chest.

He said very little, but his eyes were eloquent; the clutch of his arms was eloquent. He was the playground of unspeakable emotions. These, you know, were REAL Magics. Then, with a start, I discovered something moving about in my hat—something soft and jumpy. I whipped it off, and a ruffled pigeon—no doubt a confederate—dropped out and ran on the counter, and went, I fancy, into a cardboard box behind the papier-mache tiger.

'Tut, tut!' said the shopman, dexterously relieving me of my headdress; 'careless bird, and—as I live—nesting!'

He shook my hat, and shook out into his extended hand two or three eggs, a large marble, a watch, about half-a-dozen of the inevitable glass balls, and then crumpled, crinkled paper, more and more and more, talking all the time of the way in which people neglect to brush their hats INSIDE as well as out, politely, of course, but with a certain personal application. 'All sorts of things accumulate, sir.... Not YOU, of course, in particular.... Nearly every customer.... Astonishing what they carry about with them....' The crumpled paper rose and billowed on the counter more and more and more, until he was nearly hidden from us, until he was altogether hidden, and still his voice went on and on. 'We none of us know what the fair semblance of a human being may conceal, sir. Are we all then no better than brushed exteriors, whited sepulchres—'

His voice stopped—exactly like when you hit a neighbour's gramophone with a well-aimed brick, the same instant silence, and the rustle of the paper stopped, and everything was still....

'Have you done with my hat?' I said, after an interval.

There was no answer.

I stared at Gip, and Gip stared at me, and there were our distortions in the magic mirrors, looking very rum, and grave, and quiet....

'I think we'll go now,' I said. 'Will you tell me how much all this comes to?....

'I say,' I said, on a rather louder note, 'I want the bill, and my hat, please.'

It might have been a sniff from behind the paper pile....

'Let's look behind the counter, Gip,' I said. 'He's making fun of us.'

I led Gip round the head-wagging tiger, and what do you think there was behind the counter? No one at all! Only my hat on the floor, and a common conjurer's lop-eared white rabbit lost in meditation, and looking as stupid and crumpled as only a conjurer's rabbit can do. I resumed my hat, and the rabbit lolloped a lollop or so out of my way.

'Dadda!' said Gip, in a guilty whisper.

'What is it, Gip?' said I.

'I DO like this shop, dadda.'

'So should I,' I said to myself, 'if the counter wouldn't suddenly extend itself to shut one off from the door.' But I didn't call Gip's attention to that. 'Pussy!' he said, with a hand out to the rabbit as it came lolloping past us, 'Pussy, do Gip a magic!' and his eyes followed it as it squeezed through a door I had certainly not remarked a moment before. Then this door opened wider, and the man with one ear larger than the other appeared again. He was smiling still, but his eye met mine with something between amusement and defiance. 'You'd like to see our show-room, sir,' he said, with an innocent suavity. Gip tugged my finger forward. I glanced at the counter and met the shopman's eye again. I was beginning to think the magic just a little too genuine. 'We haven't VERY much time,' I said. But somehow we were inside the show-room before I could finish that.

'All goods of the same quality,' said the shopman, rubbing his flexible hands together, 'and that is the Best. Nothing in the place that isn't genuine Magic, and warranted thoroughly rum. Excuse me, sir!'

I felt him pull at something that clung to my coat-sleeve, and then I saw he held a little, wriggling red demon by the tail—the little creature bit and fought and tried to get at his hand—and in a moment he tossed it carelessly behind a counter. No doubt the thing was only an image of twisted indiarubber, and his gesture was exactly that of a man who handles some petty biting bit of vermin. I glanced at Gip, but Gip was looking at a magic rocking-horse. I was glad he hadn't seen the thing. 'I say,' I said, in an undertone, and indicating Gip and the red demon with my eyes, 'you haven't many things like THAT about, have you?'

'None of ours! Probably brought it with you,' said

the shopman—also in an undertone, and with a more dazzling smile than ever. 'Astonishing what people WILL carry about with them unawares!' And then to Gip, 'Do you see anything you fancy here?'

There were many things that Gip fancied there. He turned to this astonishing tradesman with mingled confidence and respect. 'Is that a Magic Sword?' he said.

'A Magic Toy Sword. It neither bends, breaks, nor cuts the fingers. It renders the bearer invincible in battle against any one under eighteen. Half-a-crown to seven and sixpence, according to size. These panoplies on cards are for juvenile knights-errant and very useful—shield of safety, sandals of swiftness, helmet of invisibility.'

'Oh, daddy!' gasped Gip.

I tried to find out what they cost, but the shopman did not heed me. He had got Gip now; he had got him away from my finger; he had embarked upon the exposition of all his confounded stock, and nothing was going to stop him. Presently I saw with a qualm of distrust and something very like jealousy that Gip had hold of this person's finger as usually he has hold of mine. No doubt the fellow was interesting, I thought, and had an interestingly faked lot of stuff, really GOOD faked stuff, still—

I wandered after them, saying very little, but keeping an eye on this prestidigital fellow. After all, Gip was enjoying it. And no doubt when the time came to go we should be able to go quite easily.

It was a long, rambling place, that show-room, a

gallery broken up by stands and stalls and pillars, with archways leading off to other departments, in which the queerest-looking assistants loafed and stared at one, and with perplexing mirrors and curtains. So perplexing, indeed, were these that I was presently unable to make out the door by which we had come.

The shopman showed Gip magic trains that ran without steam or clockwork, just as you set the signals, and then some very, very valuable boxes of soldiers that all came alive directly you took off the lid and said— I myself haven't a very quick ear and it was a tongue-twisting sound, but Gip—he has his mother's ear—got it in no time. 'Bravo!' said the shopman, putting the men back into the box unceremoniously and handing it to Gip. 'Now,' said the shopman, and in a moment Gip had made them all alive again.

'You'll take that box?' asked the shopman.

'We'll take that box,' said I, 'unless you charge its full value. In which case it would need a Trust Magnate—'

'Dear heart! NO!' and the shopman swept the little men back again, shut the lid, waved the box in the air, and there it was, in brown paper, tied up and—WITH GIP'S FULL NAME AND ADDRESS ON THE PAPER!

The shopman laughed at my amazement.

'This is the genuine magic,' he said. 'The real thing.'

'It's a little too genuine for my taste,' I said again.

After that he fell to showing Gip tricks, odd tricks, and still odder the way they were done. He explained them, he turned them inside out, and there was the dear little chap nodding his busy bit of a head in the sagest manner.

I did not attend as well as I might. 'Hey, presto!' said the Magic Shopman, and then would come the clear, small 'Hey, presto!' of the boy. But I was distracted by other things. It was being borne in upon me just how tremendously rum this place was; it was, so to speak, inundated by a sense of rumness. There was something a little rum about the fixtures even, about the ceiling, about the floor, about the casually distributed chairs. I had a queer feeling that whenever I wasn't looking at them straight they went askew, and moved about, and played a noiseless puss-in-the-corner behind my back. And the cornice had a serpentine design with masks—masks altogether too expressive for proper plaster.

Then abruptly my attention was caught by one of the odd-looking assistants. He was some way off and evidently unaware of my presence—I saw a sort of three-quarter length of him over a pile of toys and through an arch—and, you know, he was leaning against a pillar in an idle sort of way doing the most horrid things with his features! The particular horrid thing he did was with his nose. He did it just as though he was idle and wanted to amuse himself. First of all it was a short, blobby nose, and then suddenly he shot it out like a telescope, and then out it flew and became thinner and thinner until it was like a long, red, flexible whip. Like a thing in a nightmare it was! He flourished it about and flung it forth as a fly-fisher flings his line.

My instant thought was that Gip mustn't see him. I turned about, and there was Gip quite preoccupied with the shopman, and thinking no evil. They were whispering together and looking at me. Gip was standing on a little stool, and the shopman was holding a sort of big drum in his hand.

'Hide and seek, dadda!' cried Gip. 'You're He!'

And before I could do anything to prevent it, the shopman had clapped the big drum over him. I saw what was up directly. 'Take that off,' I cried, 'this instant! You'll frighten the boy. Take it off!'

The shopman with the unequal ears did so without a word, and held the big cylinder towards me to show its emptiness. And the little stool was vacant! In that instant my boy had utterly disappeared?...

You know, perhaps, that sinister something that comes like a hand out of the unseen and grips your heart about. You know it takes your common self away and leaves you tense and deliberate, neither slow nor hasty, neither angry nor afraid. So it was with me.

I came up to this grinning shopman and kicked his stool aside.

'Stop this folly!' I said. 'Where is my boy?'

'You see,' he said, still displaying the drum's interior, 'there is no deception—-'

I put out my hand to grip him, and he eluded me by a dexterous movement. I snatched again, and he turned from me and pushed open a door to escape. 'Stop!' I said, and he laughed, receding. I leapt after him—into utter darkness.

THUD!

'Lor' bless my 'eart! I didn't see you coming, sir!'

I was in Regent Street, and I had collided with a decent-looking working man; and a yard away, perhaps, and looking a little perplexed with himself, was Gip. There was some sort of apology, and then Gip had turned and come to me with a bright little smile, as though for a moment he had missed me.

And he was carrying four parcels in his arm!

He secured immediate possession of my finger.

For the second I was rather at a loss. I stared round to see the door of the magic shop, and, behold, it was not there! There was no door, no shop, nothing, only the common pilaster between the shop where they sell pictures and the window with the chicks!

I did the only thing possible in that mental tumult; I walked straight to the kerbstone and held up my umbrella for a cab.

"Ansoms,' said Gip, in a note of culminating exultation.

I helped him in, recalled my address with an effort, and got in also. Something unusual proclaimed itself in my tail-coat pocket, and I felt and discovered a glass ball. With a petulant expression I flung it into the street.

Gip said nothing.

For a space neither of us spoke.

'Dada!' said Gip, at last, 'that WAS a proper shop!'

I came round with that to the problem of just how the whole thing had seemed to him. He looked completely undamaged—so far, good; he was neither scared nor unhinged, he was simply tremendously satisfied with the afternoon's entertainment, and there in his arms were the four parcels.

Confound it! what could be in them?

'Um!' I said. 'Little boys can't go to shops like that every day.'

He received this with his usual stoicism, and for a moment I was sorry I was his father and not his mother, and so couldn't suddenly there, coram publico, in our hansom, kiss him. After all, I thought, the thing wasn't so very bad.

But it was only when we opened the parcels that I really began to be reassured. Three of them contained boxes of soldiers, quite ordinary lead soldiers, but of so good a quality as to make Gip altogether forget that originally these parcels had been Magic Tricks of the only genuine sort, and the fourth contained a kitten, a little living white kitten, in excellent health and appetite and temper.

I saw this unpacking with a sort of provisional relief. I hung about in the nursery for quite an unconscionable time....

That happened six months ago. And now I am beginning to believe it is all right. The kitten had only the magic natural to all kittens, and the soldiers seem as steady a company as any colonel could desire. And Gip—?

The intelligent parent will understand that I have to go cautiously with Gip.

But I went so far as this one day. I said, 'How would you like your soldiers to come alive, Gip, and march about by themselves?'

'Mine do,' said Gip. 'I just have to say a word I know before I open the lid.'

'Then they march about alone?'

'Oh, QUITE, dadda. I shouldn't like them if they didn't do that.'

I displayed no unbecoming surprise, and since then I have taken occasion to drop in upon him once or twice, unannounced, when the soldiers were about, but so far I have never discovered them performing in anything like a magical manner.

It's so difficult to tell.

There's also a question of finance. I have an incurable habit of paying bills. I have been up and down Regent Street several times, looking for that shop. I am inclined to think, indeed, that in that matter honour is satisfied, and that, since Gip's name and address are known to them, I may very well leave it to these people, whoever they may be, to send in their bill in their own time.

the magic fish-bone

a holiday romance from the pen of miss alice rainbird aged 7

CHARLES DICKENS

There was once a King, and he had a Queen; and he was the manliest of his sex, and she was the loveliest of hers. The King was, in his private profession, Under Government. The Queen's father had been a medical man out of town.

They had nineteen children, and were always having more. Seventeen of these children took care of the baby; and Alicia, the eldest, took care of them all. Their ages varied from seven years to seven months.

Let us now resume our story.

One day the King was going to the office, when he stopped at the fishmonger's to buy a pound and a half of salmon not too near the tail, which the Queen (who was a careful housekeeper) had requested him to send home.

Mr Pickles, the fishmonger, said, 'Certainly, sir, is there any other article, Good-morning.'

The King went on towards the office in a melancholy mood, for quarter day was such a long way off, and several of the dear children were growing out of their clothes. He had not proceeded far, when Mr Pickles's errand-boy came running after him, and said, 'Sir, you didn't notice the old lady in our shop.'

'What old lady?' enquired the King. 'I saw none.'

Now, the King had not seen any old lady, because this old lady had been invisible to him, though visible to Mr Pickles's boy. Probably because he messed and splashed the water about to that degree, and flopped the pairs of soles down in that violent manner, that, if she had not been visible to him, he would have spoilt her clothes.

Just then the old lady came trotting up. She was dressed in shot-silk of the richest quality, smelling of dried lavender.

'King Watkins the First, I believe?' said the old lady.

'Watkins,' replied the King, 'is my name.'

'Papa, if I am not mistaken, of the beautiful Princess Alicia?' said the old lady.

'And of eighteen other darlings,' replied the King.

'Listen. You are going to the office,' said the old lady.

It instantly flashed upon the King that she must be a Fairy, or how could she know that?

'You are right,' said the old lady, answering his thoughts, 'I am the Good Fairy Grandmarina. Attend. When you return home to dinner, politely invite the

Princess Alicia to have some of the salmon you bought just now.'

'It may disagree with her,' said the King.

The old lady became so very angry at this absurd idea, that the King was quite alarmed, and humbly begged her pardon.

'We hear a great deal too much about this thing disagreeing, and that thing disagreeing,' said the old lady, with the greatest contempt it was possible to express. 'Don't be greedy. I think you want it all yourself.'

The King hung his head under this reproof, and said he wouldn't talk about things disagreeing, any more.

'Be good, then,' said the Fairy Grandmarina, 'and don't! When the beautiful Princess Alicia consents to partake of the salmon—as I think she will—you will find she will leave a fish-bone on her plate. Tell her to dry it, and to rub it, and to polish it till it shines like mother-of-pearl, and to take care of it as a present from me.'

'Is that all?' asked the King.

'Don't be impatient, sir,' returned the Fairy Grandmarina, scolding him severely. 'Don't catch people short, before they have done speaking. Just the way with you grown-up persons. You are always doing it.'

The King again hung his head, and said he wouldn't do so any more.

'Be good then,' said the Fairy Grandmarina, 'and don't! Tell the Princess Alicia, with my love, that the fish-bone is a magic present which can only be used once; but that it will bring her, that once, whatever she wishes for,

PROVIDED SHE WISHES FOR IT AT THE RIGHT TIME. That is the message. Take care of it.'

The King was beginning, 'Might I ask the reason—?' when the Fairy became absolutely furious.

'*Will* you be good, sir?' she exclaimed, stamping her foot on the ground. 'The reason for this, and the reason for that, indeed! You are always wanting the reason. No reason. There! Hoity toity me! I am sick of your grown-up reasons.'

The King was extremely frightened by the old lady's flying into such a passion, and said he was very sorry to have offended her, and he wouldn't ask for reasons any more.

'Be good then,' said the old lady, 'and don't!'

With those words, Grandmarina vanished, and the King went on and on and on, till he came to the office. There he wrote and wrote and wrote, till it was time to go home again. Then he politely invited the Princess Alicia, as the Fairy had directed him, to partake of the salmon. And when she had enjoyed it very much, he saw the fishbone on her plate, as the Fairy had told him he would, and he delivered the Fairy's message, and the Princess Alicia took care to dry the bone, and to rub it, and to polish it till it shone like mother-of-pearl.

And so when the Queen was going to get up in the morning, she said, 'O, dear me, dear me; my head, my head!' and then she fainted away.

The Princess Alicia, who happened to be looking in at the chamber-door, asking about breakfast, was very much alarmed when she saw her Royal Mamma in this state, and she rang the bell for Peggy, which was the name of the Lord Chamberlain. But remembering where the smelling-bottle was, she climbed on a chair and got it, and after that she climbed on another chair by the bedside and held the smelling-bottle to the Queen's nose, and after that she jumped down and got some water, and after that she jumped up again and wetted the Queen's forehead, and, in short, when the Lord Chamberlain came in, that dear old woman said to the little Princess, 'What a Trot you are! I couldn't have done it better myself.'

But that was not the worst of the good Queen's illness. O, no! She was very ill indeed, for a long time. The Princess Alicia kept the seventeen young Princes and Princesses quiet, and dressed and undressed and danced the baby, and made the kettle boil, and heated the soup, and swept the hearth, and poured out the medicine, and nursed the Queen, and did all that ever she could, and was as busy busy busy, as busy could be. For there were not many servants at that Palace, for three reasons; because the King was short of money, because a rise in his office never seemed to come, and because quarter day was so far off that it looked almost as far off and as little as one of the stars.

But on the morning when the Queen fainted away, where was the magic fish-bone? Why, there it was in the Princess Alicia's pocket. She had almost taken it out to bring the Queen to life again, when she put it back, and looked for the smelling-bottle.

After the Queen had come out of her swoon that morning, and was dozing, the Princess Alicia hurried upstairs to tell a most particular secret to a most particularly confidential friend of hers, who was a Duchess. People did suppose her to be a Doll; but she was really a Duchess, though nobody knew it except the Princess.

This most particular secret was a secret about the magic fish-bone, the history of which was well known to the Duchess, because the Princess told her everything. The Princess kneeled down by the bed on which the Duchess was lying, full-dressed and wide awake, and whispered the secret to her. The Duchess smiled and nodded. People might have supposed that she never smiled and nodded, but she often did, though nobody knew it except the Princess.

Then the Princess Alicia hurried downstairs again, to keep watch in the Queen's room. She often kept watch by herself in the Queen's room; but every evening, while the illness lasted, she sat there watching with the King. And every evening the King sat looking at her with a cross look, wondering why she never brought out the magic fish-bone. As often as she noticed this, she ran upstairs, whispered the secret to the Duchess over again, and said to the Duchess besides, 'They think we children never have a reason or a meaning!' And the Duchess, though the most fashionable Duchess that ever was heard of, winked her eye.

'Alicia,' said the King, one evening when she wished him Good Night.

'Yes, Papa.'

'What is become of the magic fish-bone?'

'In my pocket, Papa.'

'I thought you had lost it?'

'O, no, Papa.'

'Or forgotten it?'

'No, indeed, Papa.'

And so another time the dreadful little snapping pug-dog next door made a rush at one of the young Princes as he stood on the steps coming home from school, and terrified him out of his wits and he put his hand through a pane of glass, and bled bled bled. When the seventeen other young Princes and Princesses saw him bleed bleed bleed, they were terrified out of their wits too, and screamed themselves black in their seventeen faces all at once. But the Princess Alicia put her hands over all their seventeen mouths, one after another, and persuaded them to be quiet because of the sick Queen. And then she put the wounded Prince's hand in a basin of fresh cold water, while they stared with their twice seventeen are thirty-four put down four and carry three eyes, and then she looked in the hand for bits of glass, and there were fortunately no bits of glass there. And then she said to two chubby-legged Princes who were sturdy though small, 'Bring me in the Royal rag-bag; I must snip and stitch and cut and contrive.' So those two young Princes tugged at the Royal rag-bag and lugged it in, and the Princess Alicia sat down on the floor with a large pair of scissors and a needle and thread, and snipped and stitched and cut and contrived, and made a bandage and put it on, and it fitted beautifully, and so when it was all done she saw the King her Papa looking on by the door.

'Alicia.'

'Yes, Papa.'

'What have you been doing?'

'Snipping stitching cutting and contriving, Papa.'

'Where is the magic fish-bone?'

'In my pocket, Papa.'

'I thought you had lost it?'

'O, no, Papa.'

'Or forgotten it?'

'No, indeed, Papa.' After that, she ran upstairs to the Duchess and told her what had passed, and told her the secret over again, and the Duchess shook her flaxen curls and laughed with her rosy lips.

Well! and so another time the baby fell under the grate. The seventeen young Princes and Princesses were used to it, for they were almost always falling under the grate or down the stairs, but the baby was not used to it yet, and it gave him a swelled face and a black eye. The way the poor little darling came to tumble was, that he slid out of the Princess Alicia's lap just as she was sitting in a great coarse apron that quite smothered her, in front of the kitchen-fire, beginning to peel the turnips for the broth for dinner; and the way she came to be doing that was, that the King's cook had run away that morning with her own true love who was a very tall but very tipsy soldier. Then, the seventeen young Princes and

Princesses, who cried at everything that happened, cried and roared. But the Princess Alicia (who couldn't help crying a little herself) quietly called to them to be still, on account of not throwing back the Queen upstairs, who was fast getting well, and said, 'Hold your tongues, you wicked little monkeys, every one of you, while I examine Baby!' Then she examined Baby, and found that he hadn't broken anything, and she held cold iron to his poor dear eye, and smoothed his poor dear face, and he presently fell asleep in her arms. Then, she said to the seventeen Princes and Princesses, 'I am afraid to lay him down yet, lest he should wake and feel pain, be good, and you shall all be cooks.' They jumped for joy when they heard that, and began making themselves cooks' caps out of old newspapers. So to one she gave the salt-box, and to one she gave the barley, and to one she gave the herbs, and to one she gave the turnips, and to one she gave the carrots, and to one she gave the onions, and to one she gave the spice-box, till they were all cooks, and all running about at work, she sitting in the middle smothered in the great coarse apron, nursing Baby. By and by the broth was done, and the baby woke up smiling like an angel, and was trusted to the sedatest Princess to hold, while the other Princes and Princesses were squeezed into a far-off corner to look at the Princess Alicia turning out the saucepan-full of broth, for fear (as they were always getting into trouble) they should get splashed and scalded. When the broth came tumbling out, steaming beautifully, and smelling like a nosegay good to eat, they clapped their hands. That made the baby clap his hands; and that, and his looking as if he had a comic toothache, made all the Princes and Princesses laugh. So the Princess Alicia said, 'Laugh and be good, and after dinner we will make him a nest on the floor in a corner, and he shall sit in his nest and see a dance of eighteen cooks.' That delighted the young Princes and Princesses, and they ate up all the broth, and washed up all the plates and dishes, and cleared away, and pushed the table into a corner, and then they in their cooks' caps, and the Princess Alicia in the smothering coarse apron that belonged to the cook that had run away with her own true love that was the very tall but very tipsy soldier, danced a dance of eighteen cooks before the angelic baby, who forgot his swelled face and his black eye, and crowed with joy.

And so then, once more the Princess Alicia saw King Watkins the First, her father, standing in the doorway looking on, and he said: 'What have you been doing, Alicia?'

'Cooking and contriving, Papa.'

'What else have you been doing, Alicia?'

'Keeping the children light-hearted, Papa.'

'Where is the magic fish-bone, Alicia?'

'In my pocket, Papa.'

'I thought you had lost it?'

'O, no, Papa.'

'Or forgotten it?'

'No, indeed, Papa.'

The King then sighed so heavily, and seemed so low-spirited, and sat down so miserably, leaning his head upon his hand, and his elbow upon the kitchen table pushed away in the corner, that the seventeen Princes and Princesses crept softly out of the kitchen, and left him alone with the Princess Alicia and the angelic baby.

'What is the matter, Papa?'

'I am dreadfully poor, my child.'

'Have you no money at all, Papa?'

'None my child.'

'Is there no way left of getting any, Papa?'

'No way,' said the King. 'I have tried very hard, and I have tried all ways.'

When she heard those last words, the Princess Alicia began to put her hand into the pocket where she kept the magic fish-bone.

'Papa,' said she, 'when we have tried very hard, and tried all ways, we must have done our very very best?'

'No doubt, Alicia.'

'When we have done our very very best, Papa, and that is not enough, then I think the right time must have come for asking help of others.' This was the very secret connected with the magic fish-bone, which she had found out for herself from the good fairy Grandmarina's words, and which she had so often whispered to her beautiful and fashionable friend the Duchess.

So she took out of her pocket the magic fish-bone that had been dried and rubbed and polished till it shone like mother-of-pearl; and she gave it one little kiss and wished it was quarter day. And immediately it *was* quarter day;

and the King's quarter's salary came rattling down the chimney, and bounced into the middle of the floor.

But this was not half of what happened, no not a quarter, for immediately afterwards the good fairy Grandmarina came riding in, in a carriage and four (Peacocks), with Mr Pickles's boy up behind, dressed in silver and gold, with a cocked hat, powdered hair, pink silk stockings, a jewelled cane, and a nosegay. Down jumped Mr Pickles's boy with his cocked hat in his hand and wonderfully polite (being entirely changed by enchantment), and handed Grandmarina out, and there she stood in her rich shot silk smelling of dried lavender, fanning herself with a sparkling fan.

'Alicia, my dear,' said this charming old Fairy, 'how do you do, I hope I see you pretty well, give me a kiss.'

The Princess Alicia embraced her, and then Grandmarina turned to the King, and said rather sharply, 'Are you good?'

The King said he hoped so.

'I suppose you know the reason, now, why my goddaughter here,' kissing the Princess again, 'did not apply to the fish-bone sooner?' said the Fairy.

The King made her a shy bow.

'Ah! but you didn't then!' said the Fairy.

The King made her a shyer bow.

'Any more reasons to ask for?' said the Fairy.

The King said no, and he was very sorry.

'Be good then,' said the Fairy, 'and live happy ever afterwards.'

Then, Grandmarina waved her fan, and the Queen came in most splendidly dressed, and the seventeen young Princes and Princesses, no longer grown out of their clothes, came in newly fitted out from top to toe, with tucks in everything to admit of its being let out. After that, the Fairy tapped the Princess Alicia with her fan, and the smothering coarse apron flew away, and she appeared exquisitely dressed, like a little Bride, with a wreath of orange-flowers and a silver veil. After that, the kitchen dresser changed of itself into a wardrobe, made of beautiful woods and gold and looking glass, which was full of dresses of all sorts, all for her and all exactly fitting her. After that, the angelic baby came in, running alone, with his face and eye not a bit the worse but much the better. Then, Grandmarina begged to be introduced to the Duchess, and, when the Duchess was brought down many compliments passed between them.

A little whispering took place between the Fairy and the Duchess, and then the Fairy said out loud, 'Yes. I thought she would have told you.' Grandmarina then turned to the King and Queen, and said, 'We are going in search of Prince Certainpersonio. The pleasure of your company is requested at church in half an hour precisely.' So she and the Princess Alicia got into the carriage, and Mr Pickles's boy handed in the Duchess who sat by herself on the opposite seat, and then Mr Pickles's boy put up the steps and got up behind, and the Peacocks flew away with their tails spread.

Prince Certainpersonio was sitting by himself, eating

barley-sugar and waiting to be ninety. When he saw the Peacocks followed by the carriage, coming in at the window, it immediately occurred to him that something uncommon was going to happen.

'Prince,' said Grandmarina, 'I bring you your Bride.'

The moment the Fairy said those words, Prince Certainpersonio's face left off being stickey, and his jacket and corduroys changed to peach-bloom velvet, and his hair curled, and a cap and feather flew in like a bird and settled on his head. He got into the carriage by the Fairy's invitation, and there he renewed his acquaintance with the Duchess, whom he had seen before.

In the church were the Prince's relations and friends, and the Princess Alicia's relations and friends, and the seventeen Princes and Princesses, and the baby, and a crowd of the neighbours. The marriage was beautiful beyond expression. The Duchess was bridesmaid, and beheld the ceremony from the pulpit where she was supported by the cushion of the desk.

Grandmarina gave a magnificent wedding feast afterwards, in which there was everything and more to eat, and everything and more to drink. The wedding cake was delicately ornamented with white satin ribbons, frosted silver and white lilies, and was forty-two yards round.

When Grandmarina had drunk her love to the young couple, and Prince Certainpersonio had made a speech, and everybody had cried Hip hip hip hurrah! Grandmarina announced to the King and Queen that in future there would be eight quarter days in every year, except in leap year, when there would be ten. She then turned to Certainpersonio and Alicia, and said, 'My dears, you will have thirty-five children, and they will all be good and beautiful. Seventeen of your children will be boys, and eighteen will be girls. The hair of the whole of your children will curl naturally. They will never have the measles, and will have recovered from the whooping-cough before being born.'

On hearing such good news, everybody cried out 'Hip hip hip hurrah!' again.

'It only remains,' said Grandmarina in conclusion, 'to make an end of the fish-bone.'

So she took it from the hand of the Princess Alicia, and it instantly flew down the throat of the dreadful little snapping pug-dog next door and choked him, and he expired in convulsions.

the nursery alice

LEWIS CARROLL

I
THE WHITE RABBIT

Once upon a time, there was a little girl called Alice: and she had a very curious dream.

Would you like to hear what it was that she dreamed about?

Well, this was the *first* thing that happened. A White Rabbit came running by, in a great hurry; and, just as it passed Alice, it stopped, and took its watch out of its pocket.

Wasn't *that* a funny thing? Did *you* ever see a Rabbit that had a watch, and a pocket to put it in? Of course, when a

Rabbit has a watch, it *must* have a pocket to put it in: it would never do to carry it about in its mouth—and it wants its hands sometimes, to run about with.

Hasn't it got pretty pink eyes (I think *all* White Rabbits have pink eyes); and pink ears; and a nice brown coat; and you can just see its red pocket-handkerchief peeping out of its coat-pocket: and, what with its blue neck-tie and its yellow waistcoat, it really is *very* nicely dressed.

'Oh dear, oh dear!' said the Rabbit. 'I shall be too late!' *What* would it be too late *for*, I wonder? Well, you see, it had to go and visit the Duchess (you'll see a picture of the Duchess, soon, sitting in her kitchen): and the Duchess was a very cross old lady: and the Rabbit *knew* she'd be very angry indeed if he kept her waiting. So the poor thing was as frightened as frightened could be (Don't you see how he's trembling? Just shake the book a little, from side to side, and you'll soon see him tremble), because he thought the Duchess would have his head cut off, for a punishment. That was what the Queen of Hearts used to do, when *she* was angry with people (you'll see a picture of *her*, soon): at least she used to *order* their heads to be cut off, and she always *thought* it was done, though they never *really* did it.

And so, when the White Rabbit ran away, Alice wanted to see what would happen to it: so she ran after it: and she ran, and she ran, till she tumbled right down the rabbit-hole.

And then she had a very long fall indeed. Down, and down, and down, till she began to wonder if she was going right *through* the World, so as to come out on the other side!

It was just like a very deep well: only there was no water in it. If anybody *really* had such a fall as that, it would kill them, most likely: but you know it doesn't hurt a bit to fall in a *dream*, because, all the time you *think* you're falling, you really *are* lying somewhere, safe and sound, and fast asleep!

However, this terrible fall came to an end at last, and down came Alice on a heap of sticks and dry leaves. But she wasn't a bit hurt, and up she jumped, and ran after the Rabbit again.

And so that was the beginning of Alice's curious dream. And, next time you see a White Rabbit, try and fancy *you're* going to have a curious dream, just like dear little Alice.

II
HOW ALICE GREW TALL

And so, after Alice had tumbled down the rabbit-hole, and had run a long long way underground, all of a sudden she found herself in a great hall, with doors all round it.

But all the doors were locked: so, you see, poor Alice couldn't get out of the hall: and that made her very sad.

However, after a little while, she came to a little table, all made of glass, with three legs (There are *two* of the legs in the picture, and just the *beginning* of the other leg, do you see?), and on the table was a little key: and she went

round the hall, and tried if she could unlock any of the doors with it.

Poor Alice! The key wouldn't unlock *any* of the doors. But at last she came upon a tiny little door: and oh, how glad she was, when she found the key would fit it!

So she unlocked the tiny little door, and she stooped down and looked through it, and what do you think she saw? Oh, such a beautiful garden! And she did so *long* to go into it! But the door was *far* too small. She couldn't squeeze herself through, any more than *you* could squeeze yourself into a mouse-hole!

So poor little Alice locked up the door, and took the key back to the table again: and *this* time she found quite a new thing on it (now look at the picture again), and what do you think it was? It was a little bottle, with a label tied to it, with the words 'DRINK ME' on the label.

So she tasted it: and it was *very* nice: so she set to work, and drank it up. And then *such* a curious thing happened to her! You'll never guess what it was: so I shall have to tell you. She got smaller, and smaller, till at last she was just the size of a little doll!

Then she said to herself, '*Now* I'm the right size to get through the little door!' And away she ran. But, when she got there, the door was locked, and the key was on the top of the table, and she couldn't reach it! *Wasn't* it a pity she had locked up the door again?

Well, the next thing she found was a little cake: and it had the words 'EAT ME' marked on it. So of course she set to work and ate it up. And *then* what do you think happened to her? No, you'll never guess! I shall have to tell you again.

She grew, and she grew, and she grew. Taller than she was before! Taller than *any* child! Taller than any grown-up person! Taller, and taller, and taller! Just look at the picture, and you'll *see* how tall she got!

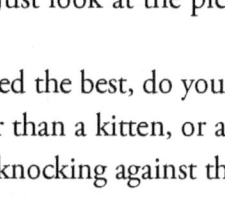

Which would *you* have liked the best, do you think, to be a little tiny Alice, no larger than a kitten, or a great tall Alice, with your head always knocking against the ceiling?

III
THE POOL OF TEARS

Perhaps you think Alice must have been very much pleased, when she had eaten the little cake, to find herself growing so tremendously tall? Because of course it would be easy enough, *now*, to reach the little key off the glass table, and to open the little tiny door.

Well, of course she could do *that*: but what good was it to get the door open, when she couldn't get *through*? She was worse off than ever, poor thing! She could just manage, by putting her head down, close to the ground, to *look* through with one eye! But that was *all* she could do. No wonder the poor tall child sat down and cried as if her heart would break.

So she cried, and she cried. And her tears ran down the middle of the hall, like a deep river. And very soon there was quite a large Pool of Tears, reaching halfway down the hall.

And there she might have stayed, till this very day, if the White Rabbit hadn't happened to come through the hall, on his way to visit the Duchess. He was dressed up as grand as grand could be, and he had a pair of white kid gloves in one hand, and a little fan in the other hand: and he kept on muttering to himself, 'Oh, the Duchess, the Duchess! Oh, *won't* she be savage if I've kept her waiting!'

But he didn't see Alice, you know. So, when she began to say, 'If you please, Sir—' her voice seemed to come from the top of the hall, because her head was so high up. And the Rabbit was dreadfully frightened: and he dropped the gloves and the fan, and ran away as hard as he could go.

Then a *very* curious thing indeed happened. Alice took up the fan, and began to fan herself with it: and, lo and behold, she got quite small again, and, all in a minute, she was just about the size of a mouse!

Now look at the picture, and you'll soon guess what happened next. It looks just like the sea, doesn't it? But it *really* is the Pool of Tears—all made of *Alice's* tears, you know!

And Alice has tumbled into the Pool: and the Mouse has tumbled in: and there they are, swimming about together.

Doesn't Alice look pretty, as she swims across the picture? You can just see her blue stockings, far away under the water.

But why is the Mouse swimming away from Alice in such a hurry? Well, the reason is, that Alice began talking about cats and dogs: and a Mouse always *hates* talking about cats and dogs!

Suppose *you* were swimming about, in a Pool of your own Tears: and suppose somebody began talking to *you* about lesson-books and bottles of medicine, wouldn't *you* swim away as hard as you could go?

IV
THE CAUCUS-RACE

When Alice and the Mouse had got out of the Pool of Tears, of course they were very wet: and so were a lot of other curious creatures, that had tumbled in as well. There was a Dodo (that's the great bird, in front, leaning on a walking-stick); and a Duck; and a Lory (that's just behind the Duck, looking over its head); and an Eaglet (that's on the left-hand side of the Lory); and several others.

Well, and so they didn't know how in the world they were to get dry again. But the Dodo—who was a very wise bird—told them the right way was to have a Caucus-Race. And what do you think *that* was?

You don't know? Well, you *are* an ignorant child! Now, be very attentive, and I'll soon cure you of your ignorance!

First, you must have a *racecourse*. It ought to be a *sort* of circle, but it doesn't much matter *what* shape it is, so long as it goes a good way round, and joins on to itself again.

Then, you must put all the *racers* on the course, here and there: it doesn't matter *where*, so long as you don't crowd them too much together.

Then, you needn't say, 'One, two, three, and away!' but let them all set off running just when they like, and leave off just when they like.

So all these creatures, Alice and all, went on running round and round, till they were all quite dry again. And then the Dodo said *everybody* had won, and *everybody* must have prizes!

Of course *Alice* had to give them their prizes. And she had nothing to give them but a few comfits she happened to have in her pocket. And there was just one a-piece, all round. And there was no prize for Alice!

So what do you think they did? Alice had nothing left but her thimble. Now look at the picture, and you'll see what happened.

'Hand it over here!' said the Dodo.

Then the Dodo took the thimble and handed it back to Alice, and said, 'We beg your acceptance of this elegant thimble!' And then all the other creatures cheered.

Wasn't *that* a curious sort of present to give her? Suppose they wanted to give *you* a birthday-present, would you rather they should go to your toy-cupboard, and pick out your nicest doll, and say, 'Here, my love, here's a lovely birthday-present for you!' or would you like them to give you something *new*, something that *didn't* belong to you before?

V
BILL, THE LIZARD

Now I'm going to tell you about Alice's Adventures in the White Rabbit's house.

Do you remember how the Rabbit dropped his gloves and his fan, when he was so frightened at hearing Alice's voice, that seemed to come down from the sky? Well, of course he couldn't go to visit the Duchess *without* his gloves and his fan: so, after a bit, he came back again to look for them.

By this time the Dodo and all the other curious creatures had gone away, and Alice was wandering about all alone.

So what do you think he did? Actually he thought she was his housemaid, and began ordering her about! 'Mary Ann!' he said. 'Go home this very minute, and fetch me a pair of gloves and a fan! Quick, now!'

Perhaps he couldn't see very clearly with his pink eyes: for I'm sure Alice doesn't look very *like* a housemaid, *does* she? However she was a very good-natured little girl: so she wasn't a bit offended, but ran off to the Rabbit's house as quick as she could.

It was lucky she found the door open: for, if she had had to ring, I suppose the *real* Mary Ann would have come to open the door: and she would *never* have let

Alice come in. And I'm sure it was *very* lucky she didn't meet the real Mary Ann, as she trotted upstairs: for I'm afraid she would have taken Alice for a robber!

So at last she found her way into the Rabbit's room: and there was a pair of gloves lying on the table, and she was just going to take them up and go away, when she happened to see a little bottle on the table. And of course it had the words 'DRINK ME!' on the label. And of course Alice drank some!

Well, I think that was *rather* lucky, too: don't *you*? For, if she *hadn't* drunk any, all this wonderful adventure, that I'm going to tell you about, wouldn't have happened at all. And wouldn't *that* have been a pity?

You're getting so used to Alice's Adventures, that I dare say you can guess what happened next? If you can't, I'll tell you.

She grew, and she grew, and she grew. And in a very short time the room was full of *Alice*: just in the same way as a jar is full of jam! There was *Alice* all the way up to the ceiling: and *Alice* in every corner of the room!

The door opened inwards: so of course there wasn't any room

to open it: so when the Rabbit got tired of waiting, and came to fetch his gloves for himself, of course he couldn't get in.

So what do you think he did? (Now we come to the picture). He sent Bill, the Lizard, up to the roof of the house, and told him to get down the chimney. But Alice happened to have one of her feet in the fire-place: so, when she heard Bill coming down the chimney, she just gave a little tiny kick, and away went Bill, flying up into the sky!

Poor little Bill! Don't you pity him very much? How frightened he must have been!

VI
THE DEAR LITTLE PUPPY

Well, it doesn't look such a very *little* Puppy, does it? But then, you see, Alice had grown very small indeed: and *that's* what makes the Puppy look so large. When Alice had eaten one of those little magic cakes, that she found in the White Rabbit's house, it made her get quite small, directly, so that she could get through the door: or else she could *never* have got out of the house again. Wouldn't *that* have been a pity? Because then she wouldn't have dreamed all the other curious things that we're going to read about.

So it really *was* a *little* Puppy, you see. And isn't it a little *pet*? And look at the way it's barking at the little stick that Alice is holding out for it! You can see she was a *little* afraid of it, all the time, because she's got behind that great thistle, for fear it should run over her. That would have been just about as bad, for *her*, as it would be for *you* to be run over by a waggon and four horses!

Have you got a little pet puppy at *your* home? If you have, I hope you're always kind to it, and give it nice things to eat.

Once upon a time, I knew some little children, about as big as you; and they had a little pet dog of their own; and it was called *Dash*. And this is what they told me about its birthday-treat.

'Do you know, one day we remembered it was Dash's birthday that day. So we said, "Let's give Dash a nice birthday-treat, like what we have on *our* birthdays!" So we thought and we thought, "Now, what is it *we* like best of all, on *our* birthdays?" And we thought and we thought. And at last we all called out together, "Why, it's *oatmeal-porridge*, of course!" So of course we thought Dash would be *quite* sure to like it very much, too.

'So we went to the cook, and we got her to make a saucerful of nice oatmeal-porridge. And then we called Dash into the house, and we said, "Now, Dash, you're going to have your birthday-treat!" We expected Dash would jump for joy: but it didn't, one bit!

'So we put the saucer down before it, and we said, "Now, Dash, don't be greedy! Eat it nicely, like a good dog!"

'So Dash just tasted it with the tip of its tongue: and then it made, oh, such a horrid face! And then, do you know, it did *hate* it so, it wouldn't eat a bit more of it! So we had to put it all down its throat with a spoon!'

I wonder if Alice will give *this* little Puppy some porridge? I don't think she *can*, because she hasn't got any with her. I can't see any saucer in the picture.

VII
THE BLUE CATERPILLAR

Would you like to know what happened to Alice, after she had got away from the Puppy? It was far too large an animal, you know, for *her* to play with. (I don't suppose *you* would much enjoy playing with a young Hippopotamus, would you? You would always be expecting to be crushed as flat as a pancake under its great heavy feet!) So Alice was very glad to run away, while it wasn't looking.

Well, she wandered up and down, and didn't know what in the world to do, to make herself grow up to her right size again. Of course she knew that she had to eat or drink *something*: that was the regular rule, you know: but she couldn't guess *what* thing.

However, she soon came to a great mushroom, that was so tall that she couldn't see over the top of it without standing on tip-toe. And what do you think she saw? Something that I'm sure *you* never talked to, in all your life!

It was a large Blue Caterpillar.

I'll tell you, soon, what Alice and the Caterpillar talked about: but first let us have a good look at the picture.

That curious thing, standing in front of the Caterpillar, is called a 'hookah': and it's used for smoking. The smoke comes through that long tube, that winds round and round like a serpent.

And do you see its long nose and chin? At least, they *look* exactly like a nose and chin, don't they? But they really *are* two of its legs. You know a Caterpillar has got *quantities* of legs: you can see some more of them, further down.

What a bother it must be to a Caterpillar, counting over such a lot of legs, every night, to make sure it hasn't lost any of them!

And *another* great bother must be, having to settle *which* leg it had better move first. I think, if *you* had forty or fifty legs, and if you wanted to go a walk, you'd be such a time in settling which leg to begin with, that you'd never go a walk at all!

And what did Alice and the Caterpillar *talk* about, I wonder?

Well, Alice told it how *very* confusing it was, being first one size and then another.

And the Caterpillar asked her if she liked the size she was, just then.

And Alice said she would like to be just a *little* bit larger—three inches was such a *wretched* height to be! (Just mark off three inches on the wall, about the length of your middle finger, and you'll see what size she was.)

And the Caterpillar told her one side of the mushroom would make her grow *taller*, and the other side would make her grow *shorter*.

So Alice took two little bits of it with her to nibble, and managed to make herself quite a nice comfortable height, before she went on to visit the Duchess.

VIII
THE PIG-BABY

Would you like to hear about Alice's visit to the Duchess? It was a very interesting visit indeed, I can assure you.

Of course she knocked at the door to begin with: but nobody came: so she had to open it for herself.

Now, if you look at the picture, you'll see exactly what Alice saw when she got inside.

The door led right into the kitchen, you see. The Duchess sat in the middle of the room, nursing the Baby. The Baby was howling. The soup was boiling. The Cook was stirring the soup. The Cat—it was a *Cheshire* Cat— was grinning, as Cheshire Cats always do. All these things were happening just as Alice went in.

The Duchess has a beautiful cap and gown, hasn't she? But I'm afraid she *hasn't* got a very beautiful *face*.

The Baby—well, I daresay you've seen *several* nicer babies than *that*: and more good-tempered ones, too. However, take a good look at it, and we'll see if you know it again, next time you meet it!

The Cook—well, you *may* have seen nicer cooks, once or twice.

But I'm nearly sure you've *never* seen a nicer *Cat*! Now *have* you? And *wouldn't* you like to have a Cat of your own, just like that one, with lovely green eyes, and smiling so sweetly?

The Duchess was very rude to Alice. And no wonder. Why, she even called her own *Baby* 'Pig'! And it *wasn't* a Pig, *was* it? And she ordered the Cook to chop off Alice's head: though of course the Cook didn't do it: and at last she threw the Baby at her! So Alice caught the Baby, and took it away with her: and I think that was about the best thing she could do.

So she wandered away, through the wood, carrying the ugly little thing with her. And a great job it was to keep hold of it, it wriggled about so. But at last she found out that the *proper* way was, to keep tight hold of its left foot and its right ear.

But don't *you* try to hold on to a Baby like that, my Child! There are not many babies that *like* being nursed in *that* way!

Well, and so the Baby kept grunting, and grunting so that Alice had to say to it, quite seriously, 'If you're going to turn into a *Pig*, my dear, I'll have nothing more to do with you. Mind now!'

And at last she looked down into its face, and what *do* you think had happened to it? Look at the picture, and see if you can guess.

'Why, *that's* not the Baby that Alice was nursing, is it?'

Ah, I *knew* you wouldn't know it again, though I told you to take a good look at it! Yes, it *is* the Baby. And it's turned into a little *Pig*!

So Alice put it down, and let it trot away into the wood. And she said to herself, 'It was a *very* ugly *Baby*: but it makes rather a handsome *Pig*, I think.'

Don't you think she was right?

IX
THE CHESHIRE-CAT

All alone, all alone! Poor Alice! No Baby, not even a *Pig* to keep her company!

So you may be sure she was very glad indeed, when she saw the Cheshire-Cat, perched up in a tree, over her head.

The Cat has a very nice smile, no doubt: but just look what a lot of teeth it's got! Isn't Alice just a *little* shy of it?

Well, yes, a *little*. But then, it couldn't help having teeth, you know: and it *could* have helped smiling, supposing it had been cross. So, on the whole, she was *glad*.

Doesn't Alice look very prim, holding her head so straight up, and with her hands behind her, just as if she were going to say her lessons to the Cat! And that reminds me. There's a little lesson I want to teach *you*, while we're looking at this picture of Alice and the Cat. Now don't be in a bad temper about it, my dear Child! It's a very *little* lesson indeed!

Do you see that Fox-Glove growing close to the tree? And do you know why it's called a *Fox*-Glove? Perhaps you think it's got something to do with a Fox? No indeed! *Foxes* never wear Gloves!

The right word is '*Folk's*-Gloves'. Did you ever hear that Fairies used to be called 'the good *Folk*'?

Now we've finished the lesson, and we'll wait a minute, till you've got your temper again.

Well? Do you feel quite good-natured again? No temper-ache? No crossness about the corners of the mouth? Then we'll go on.

'Cheshire Puss!' said Alice. (*Wasn't* that a pretty name for a Cat?) 'Would you tell me which way I ought to go from here?'

And so the Cheshire-Cat told her which way she ought to go, if she wanted to visit the Hatter, and which way to go, to visit the March Hare. 'They're both mad!' said the Cat.

And then the Cat vanished away, just like the flame of a candle when it goes out!

So Alice set off, to visit the March Hare. And as she went along, there was the Cat again! And she told it she didn't *like* it coming and going so quickly.

So this time the Cat vanished quite slowly, beginning with the tail, and ending with the grin. Wasn't *that* a curious thing, a Grin without any Cat? Would you like to see one?

X
THE MAD TEA-PARTY

This is the Mad Tea-Party. You see Alice had left the Cheshire-Cat, and had gone off to see the March Hare and the Hatter, as the Cheshire-Cat had advised her: and she found them having tea under a great tree, with a Dormouse sitting between them.

There were only those three at the table, but there were quantities of tea-cups set all along it. You can't see all the table, you know, and even in the bit you *can* see there are nine cups, counting the one the March Hare has got in his hand.

That's the March Hare, with the long ears, and straws mixed up with his hair. The straws showed he was mad—I don't know why. Never twist up straws among *your* hair, for fear people should think you're mad!

There was a nice green arm-chair at the end of the table, that looked as if it was just meant for Alice: so she went and sat down in it.

Then she had quite a long talk with the March Hare and the Hatter. The Dormouse didn't say much. You see it was fast asleep generally, and it only just woke up for a moment, now and then.

As long as it was asleep, it was very useful to the March Hare and the Hatter, because it had a nice round soft head, just like a pillow: so they could put their elbows on it, and lean across it, and talk to each other quite comfortably. You wouldn't like people to use *your* head for a pillow, *would* you? But if you were fast asleep, like the Dormouse, you wouldn't feel it: so I suppose you wouldn't care about it.

I'm afraid they gave Alice *very* little to eat and drink. However, after a bit, she helped herself to some tea and bread-and-butter: only I don't quite see where she *got* the bread-and-butter: and she had no plate for it. Nobody seems to have a plate except the Hatter. I believe the March Hare must have had one as well: because, when they all moved one place on (that was the rule at this curious tea-party), and Alice had to go into the place of the March Hare, she found he had just upset the milk-jug into his plate. So I suppose his plate and the milk-jug are hidden behind that large tea-pot.

The Hatter used to carry about hats to sell: and even the one that he's got on his head is meant to be sold. You see it's got its price marked on it—a '10' and a '6'—that means 'ten shillings and sixpence'. Wasn't that a funny way of selling hats? And hasn't he got a beautiful neck-tie on? Such a lovely yellow tie, with large red spots.

He has just got up to say to Alice, 'Your hair wants cutting!' That was a rude thing to say, *wasn't* it? And do you think her hair *does* want cutting? *I* think it's a very pretty length—just the right length.

XI
THE QUEEN'S GARDEN

This is a little bit of the beautiful garden I told you about. You see Alice had managed at last to get quite small, so that she could go through the little door. I suppose she was about as tall as a mouse, if it stood on its hind-legs: so of course this was a *very* tiny rose-tree: and these are *very* tiny gardeners.

What funny little men they are! But *are* they men, do you think? I think they must be live cards, with just

a head, and arms, and legs, so as to *look* like little men. And what *are* they doing with that red paint, I wonder? Well, you see, this is what they told Alice. The Queen of Hearts wanted to have a *red* rose-tree just in that corner: and these poor little gardeners had made a great mistake, and had put in a *white* one instead: and they were so frightened about it, because the Queen was *sure* to be angry, and then she would order all their heads to be cut off!

She was a dreadfully savage Queen, and that was the way she always did, when she was angry with people. 'Off with their heads!' They didn't *really* cut their heads off, you know: because nobody ever obeyed her: but that was what she always *said*.

Now can't you guess what the poor little gardeners are trying to do? They're trying to paint the roses *red*, and they're in a great hurry to get it done before the Queen comes. And then *perhaps* the Queen won't find out it was a *white* rose-tree to begin with: and then *perhaps* the little men won't get their heads cut off!

You see there were *five* large white roses on the tree—such a job to get them all painted red! But they've got three and a half done, now, and if only they wouldn't stop to talk—work away, little men, *do* work away! Or the Queen will be coming before it's done! And if she finds any *white* roses on the tree, do you know what will happen? It will be 'Off with their heads!' Oh, work away, my little men! Hurry, hurry!

The Magic Shop

The Queen has come! And *isn't* she angry? Oh, my poor little Alice!

XII
THE LOBSTER-QUADRILLE

Did you ever play at Croquet? There are large wooden balls, painted with different colours, that you have to roll about; and arches of wire, that you have to send them through; and great wooden mallets, with long handles, to knock the balls about with.

Now look at the picture, and you'll see that *Alice* has just been playing a Game of Croquet.

'But she *couldn't* play, with that great red what's-its-name in her arms! Why, how could she hold the mallet?'

Why, my dear Child, that great red what's-its-name (its *real* name is '*a Flamingo*') *is* the mallet! In this Croquet-Game, the balls were live *Hedge-hogs*—you know a hedge-hog can roll itself up into a ball?—and the mallets were live *Flamingos*!

So Alice is just resting from the Game, for a minute, to have a chat with that dear old thing, the Duchess: and of course she keeps her mallet under her arm, so as not to lose it.

'But I don't think she *was* a dear old thing, one bit! To call her Baby a *Pig*, and to want to chop off Alice's head!'

Oh, that was only a joke, about chopping off Alice's head: and as to the Baby—why, it *was* a Pig, you know! And just look at her *smile*! Why, it's wider than all Alice's head: and yet you can only see half of it!

Well, they'd only had a *very* little chat, when the Queen came and took Alice away, to see the Gryphon and the Mock Turtle.

You don't know what a Gryphon is? Well! Do you know *anything*? That's the question. However, look at the picture. That creature with a red head, and red claws, and green scales, is the *Gryphon*. Now you know.

And the other's the *Mock Turtle*. It's got a calf's-head, because calf's-head is used to make *Mock Turtle Soup*. Now you know.

'But what are they *doing*, going round and round Alice like that?'

Why, I thought of *course* you'd know *that*! They're dancing *a Lobster-Quadrille*.

And next time *you* meet a Gryphon and a Mock Turtle, I dare say they'll dance it for *you*, if you ask them prettily. Only don't let them come *quite*

close, or they'll be treading on your toes, as they did on poor Alice's.

XIII
WHO STOLE THE TARTS?

Did you ever hear how the Queen of Hearts made some tarts? And can you tell me what became of them?

'Why, of *course* I can! Doesn't the song tell all about it?

> *The Queen of Hearts, she made some tarts:*
> *All on a summer day:*
> *The Knave of Hearts, he stole those tarts,*
> *And took them quite away!*'

Well, yes, the *Song* says so. But it would never do to punish the poor Knave, just because there was a *Song* about him. They had to take him prisoner, and put

chains on his wrists, and bring him before the King of Hearts, so that there might be a regular trial.

Now, if you look at the big picture, you'll see what a grand thing a trial is, when the Judge is a King!

The King is very grand, *isn't* he? But he doesn't look very *happy*.

I think that big crown, on the top of his wig, must be *very* heavy and uncomfortable. But he had to wear them *both*, you see, so that people might know he was a Judge *and* a King.

And *doesn't* the Queen look cross? She can see the dish of tarts on the table, that she had taken such trouble to make. And she can see the bad Knave (do you see the chains hanging from his wrists?) that stole them away from her: so I don't think it's any wonder if she *does* feel a *little* cross.

The White Rabbit is standing near the King, reading out the Song, to tell everybody what a bad Knave he is: and the Jury (you can just see two of them, up in the Jury-box, the Frog and the Duck) have to settle whether he's 'guilty' or 'not guilty'.

Now I'll tell you about the accident that happened to Alice.

You see, she was sitting close by the Jury-box: and she was called as a witness. You know what a 'witness' is? A 'witness' is a person who has seen the prisoner do whatever he's accused of, or at any rate knows *something* that's important in the trial.

But *Alice* hadn't seen the Queen *make* the tarts: and she hadn't seen the Knave *take* the tarts: and, in fact, she didn't know anything about it: so why in the world they wanted *her* to be a witness, I'm sure *I* can't tell you!

Anyhow, they *did* want her. And the White Rabbit blew his big trumpet, and shouted out 'Alice!' And so Alice jumped up in a great hurry. And then—

And then what *do* you think happened? Why, her skirt caught against the Jury-box, and tipped it over, and all the poor little Jurors came tumbling out of it!

Let's try if we can make out all the twelve. You know there ought to be twelve to make up a Jury. I see the Frog, and the Dormouse, and the Rat and the Ferret, and the Hedgehog, and the Lizard, and the Bantam-Cock, and the Mole, and the Duck, and the Squirrel, and a screaming bird, with a long beak, just behind the Mole.

But that only makes eleven: we must find one more creature.

Oh, do you see a little white head, coming out behind the Mole, and just under the Duck's beak? That makes up the twelve.

Mr Tenniel says the screaming bird is a *Storkling* (of course you know what *that* is?) and the little white head is a *Mouseling*. Isn't it a little *darling*?

Alice picked them all up again, very carefully, and I hope they weren't *much* hurt!

XIV
THE SHOWER OF CARDS

Oh dear, oh dear! What *is* it all about? And what's happening to Alice?

Well, I'll tell you all about it, as well I can. The way the trial ended was this. The King wanted the Jury to settle whether the Knave of Hearts was *guilty* or *not guilty*—that means that they were to settle whether *he* had stolen the Tarts, or if somebody else had taken them. But the wicked *Queen* wanted to have his *punishment* settled, first of all. That wasn't at all fair, *was* it? Because, you know, supposing he never *took* the Tarts, then of course he oughtn't to be punished. Would *you* like to be punished for something you hadn't done?

So Alice said, 'Stuff and nonsense!'

So the Queen said, 'Off with her head!' (Just what she always said, when she was angry.)

So Alice said, 'Who cares for *you*? You're nothing but a pack of cards!'

So they were *all* very angry, and flew up into the air, and came tumbling down again, all over Alice, just like a shower of rain.

And I think you'll *never* guess what happened next. The next thing was, Alice woke up out of her curious dream. And she found that the cards were only some leaves off the tree, that the wind had blown down upon her face.

Wouldn't it be a nice thing to have a curious dream, just like Alice?

The best plan is this. First lie down under a tree, and wait till a White Rabbit runs by, with a watch in his hand: then shut your eyes, and pretend to be dear little Alice.

Good-bye, Alice dear, good-bye!

ozma and the little wizard

L. FRANK BAUM

Once upon a time there lived in the beautiful Emerald City, which lies in the centre of the fairy Land of Oz, a lovely girl called Princess Ozma, who was ruler of all that country. And among those who served this girlish Ruler and lived in a cosy suite of rooms in her splendid palace, was a little, withered old man known as the Wizard of Oz.

This little Wizard could do a good many queer things in magic; but he was a kind man, with merry, twinkling eyes and a sweet smile; so, instead of fearing him because of his magic, everybody loved him.

Now, Ozma was very anxious that all her people who inhabited the pleasant Land of Oz should be happy and contented, and therefore she decided one morning to make a journey to all parts of the country, that she might discover if anything was amiss, or anyone discontented, or if there was any wrong that ought to be righted. She asked the little Wizard to accompany her and he was glad to go.

'Shall I take my bag of magic tools with me?' he asked.

'Of course,' said Ozma. 'We may need a lot of magic before we return, for we are going into strange corners of the land, where we may meet with unknown creatures and dangerous adventures.'

So the Wizard took his bag of magic tools and the two left the Emerald City and wandered over the country for many days, at last reaching a place far up in the mountains which neither of them had ever visited before. Stopping one morning at a cottage, built beside the rocky path which led into a pretty valley beyond, Ozma asked a man:

'Are you happy? Have you any complaint to make of your lot?'

And the man replied:

'We are happy except for three mischievous Imps that live in yonder valley and often come here to annoy us. If Your Highness would only drive away those Imps, I and my family would be very happy and very grateful to you.'

'Who are these bad Imps?' inquired the girl Ruler.

'One is named Olite, and one Udent and one Ertinent, and they have no respect for anyone or anything. If strangers pass through the valley the Imps jeer at them and make horrid faces and call names, and often they push travellers out of the path or throw stones at them. Whenever Imp Olite or Imp Udent or Imp Ertinent comes here to bother us, I and my family run into the house and lock all the doors and windows, and we dare not venture out again until the Imps have gone away.'

Princess Ozma was grieved to hear this report and the little Wizard shook his head gravely and said the naughty Imps deserved to be punished. They told the good man they would see what could be done to protect him and at once entered the valley to seek the dwelling place of the three mischievous creatures.

Before long they came upon three caves, hollowed from the rocks, and in front of each cave squatted a queer little dwarf. Ozma and the Wizard paused to examine them and found them well-shaped, strong and lively. They had big round ears, flat noses and wide grinning mouths, and their jet-black hair came to points on top of their heads, much resembling horns. Their clothing fitted snugly to their bodies and limbs and the Imps were so small in size that at first Ozma did not consider them at all dangerous. But one of them suddenly reached out a hand and caught the dress of the Princess, jerking it so sharply that she nearly fell down, and a moment later another Imp pushed the little Wizard so hard that he bumped against Ozma and both unexpectedly sat down upon the ground.

At this the Imps laughed boisterously and began running around in a circle and kicking dust upon the Royal Princess, who cried in a sharp voice: 'Wizard, do your duty!'

The Wizard promptly obeyed. Without rising from the ground he opened his bag, got the tools he required and muttered a magic spell.

Instantly the three Imps became three bushes—of

a thorny stubby kind—with their roots in the ground. As the bushes were at first motionless, perhaps through surprise at their sudden transformation, the Wizard and the Princess found time to rise from the ground and brush the dust off their pretty clothes. Then Ozma turned to the bushes and said:

'The unhappy lot you now endure, my poor Imps, is due entirely to your naughty actions. You can no longer annoy harmless travellers and you must remain ugly bushes, covered with sharp thorns, until you repent of your bad ways and promise to be good Imps.'

'They can't help being good now, Your Highness,' said the Wizard, who was much pleased with his work, 'and the safest plan will be to allow them always to remain bushes.'

But something must have been wrong with the Wizard's magic, or the creatures had magic of their own, for no sooner were the words spoken than the bushes began to move. At first they only waved their branches at the girl and little man, but pretty soon they began to slide over the ground, their roots dragging through the earth, and one pushed itself against the Wizard and pricked him so sharply with its thorns that he cried out: 'Ouch!' and started to run away.

Ozma followed, for the other bushes were trying to stick their thorns into her legs and one actually got so near her that it tore a great rent in her beautiful dress. The girl Princess could run, however, and she followed the fleeing Wizard until he tumbled head first over a log and rolled upon the ground. Then she sprang behind a tree and shouted: 'Quick! Transform them into something else.'

The Wizard heard, but he was much confused by his fall. Grabbing from his bag the first magical tool he could find, he transformed the bushes into three white pigs. That astonished the Imps. In the shape of pigs—fat, rolypoly and cute—they scampered off a little distance and sat down to think about their new condition.

Ozma drew a long breath and coming from behind the tree she said:

'That is much better, Wiz, for such pigs as these must be quite harmless. No one need now fear the mischievous Imps.'

'I intended to transform them into mice,' replied the Wizard, 'but in my excitement I worked the wrong magic. However, unless the horrid creatures behave themselves hereafter, they are liable to be killed and eaten. They would make good chops, sausages or roasts.'

But the Imps were now angry and had no intention of behaving. As Ozma and the little Wizard turned to resume their journey, the three pigs rushed forward, dashed between their legs, and tripped them up, so that both lost their balance and toppled over, clinging to one another. As the Wizard tried to get up, he was tripped again and fell across the back of the third pig, which carried him on a run far down the valley until it dumped the little man in the river.

Ozma had been sprawled upon the ground but found she was not hurt, so she picked herself up and ran to the assistance of the Wizard, reaching him just as he was crawling out of the river, gasping for breath and dripping with water. The girl could not help laughing at his woeful appearance. But he had no sooner wiped the wet from his eyes than one of the impish pigs tripped him again and sent him into the river for a second bath. The pigs tried to trip Ozma, too, but she ran around a stump and so managed to keep out of their way. So the Wizard scrambled out of the water again and picked up a sharp stick to defend himself. Then he mumbled a magic mutter which instantly dried his clothes, after which he hurried to assist Ozma. The pigs were afraid of the sharp stick and kept away from it.

'This won't do,' said the Princess. 'We have accomplished nothing, for the pig Imps would annoy travellers as much as the real Imps. Transform them into something else, Wiz.'

The Wizard took time to think. Then he transformed the white pigs into three blue doves.

'Doves,' said he, 'are the most harmless things in the world.'

But scarcely had he spoken when the doves flew at them and tried to peck out their eyes. When they endeavoured to shield their eyes with their hands, two of the doves bit the Wizard's fingers and another caught the pretty pink ear of the Princess in its bill and gave it such a cruel tweak that she cried out in pain and threw her skirt over her head.

'These birds are worse than pigs, Wizard,' she called to her companion. 'Nothing is harmless that is animated by impudent anger or impertinent mischief. You must transform the Imps into something that is not alive.'

The Wizard was pretty busy, just then, driving off the birds, but he managed to open his bag of magic and find a charm which instantly transformed the doves into three buttons. As they fell to the ground, he picked them up and smiled with satisfaction. The tin button was Imp Olite, the brass button was Imp Udent and the lead button was Imp Ertinent. These buttons the Wizard placed in a little box which he put in his jacket pocket.

'Now,' said he, 'the Imps cannot annoy travellers, for we shall carry them back with us to the Emerald City.'

'But we dare not use the buttons,' said Ozma, smiling once more now that the danger was over.

'Why not?' asked the Wizard. 'I intend to sew them upon my coat and watch them carefully. The spirits of the Imps are still in the buttons, and after a time they will repent and be sorry for their naughtiness. Then they will decide to be very good in the future. When they feel that way, the tin button will turn to silver and the brass to gold, while the lead button will become aluminium. I shall then restore them to their proper forms, changing their names to pretty names instead of the ugly ones they used to bear. Thereafter the three Imps will become good citizens of the Land of Oz and I think you will find they will prove faithful subjects of our beloved Princess Ozma.'

'Ah, that is magic well worthwhile,' exclaimed Ozma, well pleased. 'There is no doubt, my friend, but that you are a very clever Wizard.'

the princess and the hedge-pig

E. NESBIT

'But I don't see what we're to *do*,' said the Queen for the twentieth time.

'Whatever we do will end in misfortune,' said the King gloomily, 'you'll see it will.'

They were sitting in the honeysuckle arbour talking things over, while the nurse walked up and down the terrace with the new baby in her arms.

'Yes, dear,' said the poor Queen. 'I've not the slightest doubt I shall.'

Misfortune comes in many ways, and you can't always know beforehand that a certain way is the way misfortune will come by: but there are things misfortune comes after as surely as night comes after day. For instance, if you let all the water boil away, the kettle will have a hole burnt in it. If you leave the bath taps running and the waste-pipe closed, the stairs of your house will, sooner or later, resemble Niagara. If you leave your purse at home, you won't have it with you when you want to pay your tramfare. And if you throw lighted wax matches at your muslin curtains, your parent will most likely have to pay five pounds to the fire engines for coming round and blowing the fire out with a wet hose. Also, if you are a king and do not invite the wicked fairy to your christening parties, she will come all the same. And if you do ask the wicked fairy, she will come, and in either case it will be the worse for the new princess. So what is a poor monarch to do? Of course, there is one way out of the difficulty, and that is not to have a christening party at all. But this offends all the good fairies, and then where are you?

All these reflections had presented themselves to the minds of King Ozymandias and his Queen, and neither of them could deny that they were in a most awkward situation. They were 'talking it over' for the hundredth time on the palace terrace where the pomegranates and oleanders grew in green tubs and the marble balustrade was overgrown with roses, red and white and pink and yellow. On the lower terrace the royal nurse was walking up and down with the baby princess that all the fuss was about. The Queen's eyes followed the baby admiringly.

'The darling!' she said. 'Oh, Ozymandias, don't you sometimes wish we'd been poor people?'

'Never!' said the King decidedly.

'Well, I do,' said the Queen. 'Then we could have had just you and me and your sister at the christening, and no fear of—oh! I've thought of something.'

The King's patient expression showed that he did not think it likely that she would have thought of anything useful; but at the first five words his expression changed. You would have said that he pricked up his ears, if kings had ears that could be pricked up. What she said was—
'Let's have a secret christening.'
'How?' asked the King.
The Queen was gazing in the direction of the baby with what is called a 'faraway look' in her eyes.
'Wait a minute,' she said slowly. 'I see it all—yes—we'll have the party in the cellars—you know they're splendid.'
'My great-grandfather had them built by Lancashire men, yes,' interrupted the King.
On the lower terrace the royal nurse was walking up and down with the baby princess that all the fuss was about.
'We'll send out the invitations to look like bills. The baker's boy can take them. He's a very nice boy. He made Baby laugh yesterday when I was explaining to him about the Standard Bread. We'll just put "1 loaf 3. A remittance at your earliest convenience will oblige." That'll mean that 1 person is invited for 3 o'clock, and on the back we'll write where and why in invisible ink. Lemon juice, you know. And the baker's boy shall be told to ask to see the people—just as they do when they *really* mean earliest convenience—and then he shall just whisper: "Deadly secret. Lemon juice. Hold it to the fire," and come away. Oh, dearest, do say you approve!'

The King laid down his pipe, set his crown straight, and kissed the Queen with great and serious earnestness. 'You are a wonder,' he said. 'It is the very thing. But the baker's boy is very small. Can we trust him?'

'He is nine,' said the Queen, 'and I have sometimes thought that he must be a prince in disguise. He is so very intelligent.'

The Queen's plan was carried out. The cellars, which were really extraordinarily fine, were secretly decorated by the King's confidential man and the Queen's confidential maid and a few of *their* confidential friends whom they knew they could really trust. You would never have thought they were cellars when the decorations were finished. The walls were hung with white satin and white velvet, with wreaths of white roses, and the stone floors were covered with freshly cut turf which had white daisies, brisk and neat, growing in it.

The invitations were duly delivered by the baker's boy. On them was written in plain blue ink,

'THE ROYAL BAKERIES
1 loaf 3d.
An early remittance will oblige.'

And when the people held the letter to the fire, as they were whisperingly instructed to do by the baker's boy, they read in a faint brown writing:

'King Ozymandias and Queen Eliza invite you to the christening of their daughter Princess Ozyliza at three on Wednesday in the Palace cellars.

'*P.S.*—We are obliged to be very secret and careful because of wicked fairies, so please come disguised as a tradesman with a bill, calling for the last time before it leaves your hands.'

You will understand by this that the King and Queen were not as well off as they could wish; so that tradesmen calling at the palace with that sort of message was the last thing likely to excite remark. But as most of the King's subjects were not very well off either, this was merely a bond between the King and his people. They could sympathize with each other, and understand each other's troubles in a way impossible to most kings and most nations.

You can imagine the excitement in the families of the people who were invited to the christening party, and the interest they felt in their costumes. The Lord Chief Justice disguised himself as a shoemaker; he still had his old blue brief-bag by him, and a brief-bag and a boot-bag are very much alike. The Commander-in-Chief dressed as a dog's meat man and wheeled a barrow. The Prime Minister appeared as a tailor; this required no change of dress and only a slight change of expression. And the other courtiers all disguised themselves perfectly. So did the good fairies, who had, of course, been invited first of all. Benevola, Queen of the Good Fairies, disguised herself as a moonbeam, which can go into any palace without any questions asked. Serena, the next in command, dressed as a butterfly, and all the other fairies had disguises equally pretty and tasteful.

The Queen looked most kind and beautiful, the King very handsome and manly, and all the guests agreed that the new princess was the most beautiful baby they had ever seen in all their born days.

Everybody brought the most charming christening presents concealed beneath their disguises. The fairies gave the usual gifts—beauty, grace, intelligence, charm, and so on.

Everything seemed to be going better than well. But of course you know it wasn't. The Lord High Admiral had not been able to get a cook's dress large enough to completely cover his uniform; a bit of an epaulette had peeped out, and the wicked fairy, Malevola, had spotted it as he went past her to the palace back door, near which she had been sitting disguised as a dog without a collar hiding from the police, and enjoying what she took to be the trouble the royal household were having with their tradesmen.

Malevola almost jumped out of her dog-skin when she saw the glitter of that epaulette.

'Hullo?' she said, and sniffed quite like a dog. 'I must look into this,' said she, and disguising herself as a toad, she crept unseen into the pipe by which the copper emptied itself into the palace moat—for of course there was a copper in one of the palace cellars as there always is in cellars in the North Country.

Now this copper had been a great trial to the decorators. If there is anything you don't like about your house, you can either try to conceal it or 'make a feature of it'. And as concealment of the copper was impossible, it was decided to 'make it a feature' by covering it with green moss and planting a tree in it, a little apple tree all in bloom. It had been very much admired.

Malevola, hastily altering her disguise to that of a mole, dug her way through the earth that the copper was full of, got to the top and put out a sharp nose just as Benevola was saying in that soft voice which Malevola always thought so affected—

'The Princess shall love and be loved all her life long.'

'So she shall,' said the wicked fairy, assuming her own shape amid the screams of the audience. 'Be quiet, you silly cuckoo,' she said to the Lord Chamberlain, whose screams were specially piercing, 'or I'll give *you* a christening present too.'

Instantly there was a dreadful silence. Only Queen Eliza, who had caught up the baby at Malevola's first word, said feebly, 'Oh, *don't*, dear Malevola.'

And the King said, 'It isn't exactly a party, don't you know. Quite informal. Just a few friends dropped in, eh, what?'

'So I perceive,' said Malevola, laughing that dreadful laugh of hers which makes other people feel as though they would never be able to laugh any more. 'Well, I've dropped in too. Let's have a look at the child.'

The poor Queen dared not refuse. She tottered forward with the baby in her arms.

'Humph!' said Malevola, 'your precious daughter will have beauty and grace and all the rest of the tuppenny halfpenny rubbish those niminy-piminy minxes have given her. But she will be turned out of her kingdom. She will have to face her enemies without a single human being to stand by her, and she shall never come to her own again until she finds—' Malevola hesitated. She could not think of anything sufficiently unlikely— 'until she finds,' she repeated—

'A thousand spears to follow her to battle,' said a new voice, 'a thousand spears devoted to her and to her alone.'

A very young fairy fluttered down from the little apple tree where she had been hiding among the pink and white blossoms.

'I am very young, I know,' she said apologetically, 'and I've only just finished my last course of Fairy History. So I know that if a fairy stops more than half a second in a curse she can't go on, and someone else may finish it for her. That is so, Your Majesty, isn't it?' she said, appealing to Benevola. And the Queen of the Fairies said yes, that was the law, only it was such an old one most people had forgotten it.

'You think yourself very clever,' said Malevola, 'but as a matter of fact you're simply silly. That's the very thing I've provided against. She *can't* have anyone to stand by her in battle, so she'll lose her kingdom and everyone will be killed, and I shall come to the funeral. It will be enormous,' she added rubbing her hands at the joyous thought.

'If you've quite finished,' said the King politely, 'and if you're sure you won't take any refreshment, may I wish you a very good afternoon?' He held the door open himself, and Malevola went out chuckling. The whole of the party then burst into tears.

'Never mind,' said the King at last, wiping his eyes with the tails of his ermine. 'It's a long way off and perhaps it won't happen after all.'

But of course it did.

The King did what he could to prepare his daughter for the fight in which she was to stand alone against her enemies. He had her taught fencing and riding and shooting, both with the cross bow and the long bow, as well as with pistols, rifles, and artillery. She learned to dive and to swim, to run and to jump, to box and to wrestle, so that she grew up as strong and healthy as any young man, and could, indeed, have got the best of a fight with any prince of her own age. But the few princes who called at the palace did not come to fight the Princess, and when they heard that the Princess had no dowry except the gifts of the fairies, and also what Malevola's gift had been, they all said they had just looked in as they were passing and that they must be going now, thank you. And went.

And then the dreadful thing happened. The tradesmen, who had for years been calling for the last time before, etc., really decided to place the matter in other hands. They called in a neighbouring king who marched his army into Ozymandias's country, conquered the army—the soldiers' wages hadn't been paid for years—turned out the King and Queen, paid the tradesmen's bills, had most of the palace walls papered with the receipts, and set up housekeeping there himself.

Now when this happened the Princess was away on a visit to her aunt, the Empress of Oricalchia, half the world away, and there is no regular post between the two countries, so that when she came home, travelling with a train of fifty-four camels, which is rather slow work, and arrived at her own kingdom, she expected to find all the flags flying and the bells ringing and the streets decked in roses to welcome her home.

Instead of which nothing of the kind. The streets were all as dull as dull, the shops were closed because it was early-closing day, and she did not see a single person she knew.

She left the fifty-four camels laden with the presents her aunt had given her outside the gates, and rode alone on her own pet camel to the palace, wondering whether perhaps her father had not received the letter she had sent on ahead by carrier pigeon the day before.

And when she got to the palace and got off her camel and went in, there was a strange king on her father's throne and a strange queen sat in her mother's place at his side.

'Where's my father?' said the Princess, bold as brass, standing on the steps of the throne. 'And what are you doing there?'

'I might ask you that,' said the King. 'Who are you, anyway?'

'I am the Princess Ozyliza,' said she.

'Oh, I've heard of you,' said the King. 'You've been expected for some time. Your father's been evicted, so now you know. No, I can't give you his address.'

Just then someone came and whispered to the Queen that fifty-four camels laden with silks and velvets and monkeys and parakeets and the richest treasures of Oricalchia were outside the city gate. She put two and two together, and whispered to the King, who nodded and said:

'I wish to make a new law.'

Everyone fell flat on his face. The law is so much respected in that country.

'No one called Ozyliza is allowed to own property in this kingdom,' said the King. 'Turn out that stranger.'

So the Princess was turned out of her father's palace, and went out and cried in the palace gardens where she had been so happy when she was little.

And the baker's boy, who was now the baker's young man, came by with the standard bread and saw someone crying among the oleanders, and went to say, 'Cheer up!' to whoever it was. And it was the Princess. He knew her at once.

'Oh, Princess,' he said, 'cheer up! Nothing is ever so bad as it seems.'

'Oh, Baker's Boy,' said she, for she knew him too, 'how can I cheer up? I am turned out of my kingdom. I haven't got my father's address, and I have to face my enemies without a single human being to stand by me.'

'That's not true, at any rate,' said the baker's boy, whose name was Erinaceus, 'you've got me. If you'll let me be your squire, I'll follow you 'round the world and help you to fight your enemies.'

'You won't be let,' said the Princess sadly, 'but I thank you very much all the same.'

She dried her eyes and stood up.

'I must go,' she said, 'and I've nowhere to go to.'

Now as soon as the Princess had been turned out of the palace, the Queen said, 'You'd much better have beheaded her for treason.' And the King said, 'I'll tell the archers to pick her off as she leaves the grounds.'

So when she stood up, out there among the oleanders, someone on the terrace cried, 'There she is!' and instantly a flight of winged arrows crossed the garden. At the cry Erinaceus flung himself in front of her, clasping her in his arms and turning his back to the arrows. The Royal Archers were a thousand strong and all excellent shots. Erinaceus felt a thousand arrows sticking into his back.

'And now my last friend is dead,' cried the Princess. But being a very strong princess, she dragged him into the shrubbery out of sight of the palace, and then dragged him into the wood and called aloud on Benevola, Queen of the Fairies, and Benevola came.

'They've killed my only friend,' said the Princess, 'at least…. Shall I pull out the arrows?'

'If you do,' said the Fairy, 'he'll certainly bleed to death.'

'And he'll die if they stay in,' said the Princess.

'Not necessarily,' said the Fairy, 'let me cut them a little shorter.' She did, with her fairy pocket-knife. 'Now,' she said, 'I'll do what I can, but I'm afraid it'll be a disappointment to you both. Erinaceus,' she went on, addressing the unconscious baker's boy with the stumps of the arrows still sticking in him, 'I command you, as soon as I have vanished, to assume the form of a hedge-pig. The hedge-pig,' she exclaimed to the Princess, 'is the only nice person who can live comfortably with a thousand spikes sticking out of him. Yes, I know there are porcupines, but porcupines are vicious and ill-mannered. Good-bye!'

And with that she vanished. So did Erinaceus, and the Princess found herself alone among the oleanders; and on the green turf was a small and very prickly brown hedge-pig.

'Oh, dear!' she said, 'now I'm all alone again, and the baker's boy has given his life for mine, and mine isn't worth having.'

'It's worth more than all the world,' said a sharp little voice at her feet.

'Oh, can you talk?' she said, quite cheered.

'Why not?' said the hedge-pig sturdily, 'it's only the *form* of the hedge-pig I've assumed. I'm Erinaceus inside, all right enough. Pick me up in a corner of your mantle so as not to prick your darling hands.'

'You mustn't call names, you know,' said the Princess, 'even your hedge-pigginess can't excuse such liberties.'

'I'm sorry, Princess,' said the hedge-pig, 'but I can't

help it. Only human beings speak lies; all other creatures tell the truth. Now I've got a hedge-pig's tongue it won't speak anything but the truth. And the truth is that I love you more than all the world.'

'Well,' said the Princess thoughtfully, 'since you're a hedge-pig I suppose you may love me, and I may love you. Like pet dogs or gold-fish. Dear little hedge-pig, then!'

'Don't!' said the hedge-pig, 'remember I'm the baker's boy in my mind and soul. My hedge-pigginess is only skin-deep. Pick me up, dearest of Princesses, and let us go to seek our fortunes.'

'I think it's my parents I ought to seek,' said the Princess. 'However…'

She picked up the hedge-pig in the corner of her mantle and they went away through the wood.

They slept that night at a wood-cutter's cottage. The wood-cutter was very kind, and made a nice little box of beech-wood for the hedge-pig to be carried in, and he told the Princess that most of her father's subjects were still loyal, but that no one could fight for him because they would be fighting for the Princess too, and however much they might wish to do this, Malevola's curse assured them that it was impossible.

So the Princess put her hedge-pig in its little box and went on, looking everywhere for her father and mother, and, after more adventures than I have time to tell you, she found them at last, living in quite a poor way in a semi-detached villa at Tooting. They were very glad to see her, but when they heard that she meant to try to get back the kingdom, the King said:

'I shouldn't bother, my child, I really shouldn't. We are quite happy here. I have the pension always given to Deposed Monarchs, and your mother is becoming a really economical manager.'

The Queen blushed with pleasure, and said, 'Thank you, dear. But if you should succeed in turning that wicked usurper out, Ozyliza, I hope I shall be a better queen than I used to be. I am learning housekeeping at an evening class at the Crown-maker's Institute.'

The Princess kissed her parents and went out into the garden to think it over. But the garden was small and quite full of wet washing hung on lines. So she went into the road, but that was full of dust and perambulators. Even the wet washing was better than that, so she went back and sat down on the grass in a white alley of tablecloths and sheets, all marked with a crown in indelible ink. And she took the hedge-pig out of the box. It was rolled up in a ball, but she stroked the little bit of soft forehead that you can always find if you look carefully at a rolled-up hedge-pig, and the hedge-pig uncurled and said:

'I am afraid I was asleep, Princess dear. Did you want me?'

'You're the only person who knows all about everything,' said she. 'I haven't told father and mother about the arrows. Now what do you advise?'

Erinaceus was flattered at having his advice asked, but unfortunately he hadn't any to give.

'It's your work, Princess,' he said. 'I can only promise to do anything a hedge-pig *can* do. It's not much. Of course I could die for you, but that's so useless.'

'Quite,' said she.

'I wish I were invisible,' he said dreamily.

'Oh, where are you?' cried Ozyliza, for the hedge-pig had vanished.

'Here,' said a sharp little voice. 'You can't see me, but I can see everything I want to see. And I can see what to do. I'll crawl into my box, and you must disguise yourself as an old French governess with the best references and answer the advertisement that the wicked king put yesterday in the *Usurpers Journal*.'

The Queen helped the Princess to disguise herself, which, of course, the Queen would never have done if she had known about the arrows; and the King gave her some of his pension to buy a ticket with, so she went back quite quickly, by train, to her own kingdom.

The usurping King at once engaged the French governess to teach his cook to read French cookery books, because the best recipes are in French. Of course he had no idea that there was a princess, *the* Princess, beneath the governessial disguise. The French lessons were from 6 to 8 in the morning and from 2 to 4 in the afternoon, and all the rest of the time the governess could spend as she liked. She spent it walking about the palace gardens and talking to her invisible hedge-pig. They talked about everything under the sun, and the hedge-pig was the best of company.

'How did you become invisible?' she asked one day, and it said, 'I suppose it was Benevola's doing. Only I think everyone gets *one* wish granted if they only wish hard enough.'

On the fifty-fifth day the hedge-pig said, 'Now, Princess dear, I'm going to begin to get you back your kingdom.'

And next morning the King came down to breakfast in a dreadful rage with his face covered up in bandages.

'This palace is haunted,' he said. 'In the middle of the night a dreadful spiked ball was thrown in my face. I lighted a match. There was nothing.'

The Queen said, 'Nonsense! You must have been dreaming.'

But next morning it was her turn to come down with a bandaged face. And the night after, the King had the spiky ball thrown at him again. And then the Queen had it. And then they both had it, so that they couldn't sleep at all, and had to lie awake with nothing to think of but their wickedness. And every five minutes a very little voice whispered:

'Who stole the kingdom? Who killed the Princess?' till the King and Queen could have screamed with misery.

And at last the Queen said, 'We needn't have killed the Princess.'

And the King said, 'I've been thinking that, too.'

And next day the King said, 'I don't know that we ought to have taken this kingdom. We had a really high-class kingdom of our own.'

'I've been thinking that too,' said the Queen.

By this time their hands and arms and necks and faces and ears were very sore indeed, and they were sick with want of sleep.

'Look here,' said the King, 'let's chuck it. Let's write to Ozymandias and tell him he can take over his kingdom again. I've had jolly well enough of this.'

'Let's,' said the Queen, 'but we can't bring the Princess to life again. I do wish we could,' and she cried a little through her bandages into her egg, for it was breakfast time.

'Do you mean that,' said a little sharp voice, though there was no one to be seen in the room. The King and Queen clung to each other in terror, upsetting the urn over the toast-rack.

'Do you mean it?' said the voice again; 'answer—yes or no.'

'Yes,' said the Queen, 'I don't know who you are, but, yes, yes, yes. I can't *think* how we could have been so wicked.'

'Nor I,' said the King.

'Then send for the French governess,' said the voice.

'Ring the bell, dear,' said the Queen. 'I'm sure what it says is right. It is the voice of conscience. I've often heard *of* it, but I never heard it before.'

The King pulled the richly-jewelled bell-rope and ten magnificent green and gold footmen appeared.

'Please ask Mademoiselle to step this way,' said the Queen.

The ten magnificent green and gold footmen found the governess beside the marble basin feeding the goldfish, and, bowing their ten green backs, they gave the Queen's message. The governess, who everyone agreed, was always most obliging, went at once to the pink satin breakfast-room where the King and Queen were sitting, almost unrecognizable in their bandages.

'Yes, Your Majesties?' said she curtseying.

'The voice of conscience,' said the Queen, 'told us to send for you. Is there any recipe in the French books for bringing shot princesses to life? If so, will you kindly translate it for us?'

'There is *one*,' said the Princess thoughtfully, 'and it is quite simple. Take a king and a queen and the voice of conscience. Place them in a clean pink breakfast-room with eggs, coffee, and toast. Add a full-sized French governess. The king and queen must be thoroughly pricked and bandaged, and the voice of conscience must be very distinct.'

'Is that all?' asked the Queen.

'That's all,' said the governess, 'except that the king and queen must have two more bandages over their eyes, and keep them on till the voice of conscience has counted fifty-five very slowly.'

'If you would be so kind,' said the Queen, 'as to bandage us with our table napkins? Only be careful how you fold them, because our faces are very sore, and the royal monogram is very stiff and hard owing to its being embroidered in seed pearls by special command.'

'I will be very careful,' said the governess kindly.

The moment the King and Queen were blindfolded, the 'voice of conscience' began, 'one, two, three,' and Ozyliza tore off her disguise, and under the fussy black-and-violet-spotted alpaca of the French governess was the simple slim cloth-of-silver dress of the Princess. She stuffed the alpaca up the chimney and the grey wig into the tea-cosy, and had disposed of the mittens in the coffee-pot and the elastic-side boots in the coal-scuttle, just as the voice of conscience said—

'Fifty-three, fifty-four, fifty-five!' and stopped.

The King and Queen pulled off the bandages, and there, alive and well, with bright clear eyes and pink cheeks and a mouth that smiled, was the Princess whom they supposed to have been killed by the thousand arrows of their thousand archers.

Before they had time to say a word the Princess said:

'Good morning, Your Majesties. I am afraid you have had bad dreams. So have I. Let us all try to forget them. I hope you will stay a little longer in my palace. You are very welcome. I am so sorry you have been hurt.'

'We deserved it,' said the Queen, 'and we want to say we have heard the voice of conscience, and do please forgive us.'

'Not another word,' said the Princess, '*do* let me have some fresh tea made. And some more eggs. These are quite cold. And the urn's been upset. We'll have a new breakfast. And I *am* so sorry your faces are so sore.'

'If you kissed them,' said the voice which the King

and Queen called the voice of conscience, 'their faces would not be sore any more.'

'May I?' said Ozyliza, and kissed the King's ear and the Queen's nose, all she could get at through the bandages.

And instantly they were quite well.

They had a delightful breakfast. Then the King caused the royal household to assemble in the throne-room, and there announced that, as the Princess had come to claim the kingdom, they were returning to their own kingdom by the three-seventeen train on Thursday.

Everyone cheered like mad, and the whole town was decorated and illuminated that evening. Flags flew from every house, and the bells all rang, just as the Princess had expected them to do that day when she came home with the fifty-five camels. All the treasure these had carried was given back to the Princess, and the camels themselves were restored to her, hardly at all the worse for wear.

The usurping King and Queen were seen off at the station by the Princess, and parted from her with real affection. You see they weren't completely wicked in their hearts, but they had never had time to think before. And being kept awake at night forced them to think. And the 'voice of conscience' gave them something to think about.

They gave the Princess the receipted bills, with which most of the palace was papered, in return for board and lodging.

When they were gone a telegram was sent off.

> Ozymandias Rex, Esq.,
> Chatsworth,
> Delamere Road,
> Tooting,
> England.
> Please come home at once. Palace vacant. Tenants have left.—OZYLIZA P.

And they came immediately.

When they arrived, the Princess told them the whole story, and they kissed and praised her, and called her their deliverer and the saviour of her country.

'*I* haven't done anything,' she said. 'It was Erinaceus who did everything, and…'

'But the fairies said,' interrupted the King, who was never clever at the best of times, 'that you couldn't get the kingdom back till you had a thousand spears devoted to you, to you alone.'

'There are a thousand spears in my back,' said a little sharp voice, 'and they are all devoted to the Princess and to her alone.'

'Don't!' said the King irritably. 'That voice coming out of nothing makes me jump.'

'I can't get used to it either,' said the Queen. 'We must have a gold cage built for the little animal. But I must say I wish it was visible.'

'So do I,' said the Princess earnestly. And instantly it was. I suppose the Princess wished it very hard, for there was the hedge-pig with its long spiky body and its little pointed face, its bright eyes, its small round ears, and its sharp, turned-up nose.

It looked at the Princess but it did not speak.

'Say something *now*,' said Queen Eliza. 'I should like to *see* a hedge-pig speak.'

'The truth is, if speak I must, I must speak the truth,' said Erinaceus. 'The Princess has thrown away her life-wish to make me visible. I wish she had wished instead for something nice for herself.'

'Oh, was that my life-wish?' cried the Princess. 'I didn't know, dear Hedge-pig, I didn't know. If I'd only known, I would have wished you back into your proper shape.'

'If you had,' said the hedge-pig, 'it would have been the shape of a dead man. Remember that I have a thousand spears in my back, and no man can carry those and live.'

The Princess burst into tears.

'Oh, you can't go on being a hedge-pig forever,' she said, 'it's not fair. I can't bear it. Oh Mamma! Oh Papa! Oh Benevola!'

And there stood Benevola before them, a little dazzling figure with blue butterfly's wings and a wreath of moonshine.

'Well?' she said, 'well?'

'Oh, you know,' said the Princess, still crying. 'I've thrown away my life-wish, and he's still a hedge-pig. Can't you do *anything*!'

'*I* can't,' said the Fairy, 'but you can. Your kisses are magic kisses. Don't you remember how you cured the

King and Queen of all the wounds the hedge-pig made by rolling itself on to their faces in the night?'

'But she can't go kissing hedge-pigs,' said the Queen, 'it would be most unsuitable. Besides it would hurt her.'

But the hedge-pig raised its little pointed face, and the Princess took it up in her hands. She had long since learned how to do this without hurting either herself or it. She looked in its little bright eyes.

'I would kiss you on every one of your thousand spears,' she said, 'to give you what you wish.'

'Kiss me once,' it said, 'where my fur is soft. That is all I wish, and enough to live and die for.'

She stooped her head and kissed it on its forehead where the fur is soft, just where the prickles begin.

And instantly she was standing with her hands on a young man's shoulders and her lips on a young man's face just where the hair begins and the forehead leaves off. And all round his feet lay a pile of fallen arrows.

She drew back and looked at him.

'Erinaceus,' she said, 'you're different—from the baker's boy I mean.'

'When I was an invisible hedge-pig,' he said, 'I knew everything. Now I have forgotten all that wisdom save only two things. One is that I am a king's son. I was stolen away in infancy by an unprincipled baker, and I am really the son of that usurping King whose face I rolled on in the night. It is a painful thing to roll on your father's face when you are all spiky, but I did it, Princess, for your sake, and for my father's too.

And now I will go to him and tell him all, and ask his forgiveness.'

'You won't go away?' said the Princess. 'Ah! Don't go away. What shall I do without my hedge-pig?'

Erinaceus stood still, looking very handsome and like a prince.

'What is the other thing that you remember of your hedge-pig wisdom?' asked the Queen curiously. And Erinaceus answered, not to her but to the Princess:

'The other thing, Princess, is that I love you.'

'Isn't there a third thing, Erinaceus?' said the Princess, looking down.

'There is, but you must speak that, not I.'

'Oh,' said the Princess, a little disappointed, 'then you knew that I loved you?'

'Hedge-pigs are very wise little beasts,' said Erinaceus, 'but I only knew that when you told me.'

'I—told you?'

'When you kissed my little pointed face, Princess,' said Erinaceus, 'I knew then.'

'My goodness gracious me,' said the King.

'Quite so,' said Benevola, 'and I wouldn't ask *anyone* to the wedding.'

'Except you, dear,' said the Queen.

'Well, as I happened to be passing ... there's no time like the present,' said Benevola briskly. 'Suppose you give orders for the wedding bells to be rung now, at once!'

the story of goopy the singer and bagha the drummer

UPENDRAKISHORE RAY CHOWDHURY

Translated by Tilottama Shome

Can you sing? Let me tell you about a man who could sing only one song. His name was Goopy Kyne and his father's name was Kanu Kyne. Kanu had a grocer's shop. Goopy could sing just that one song though nobody else in that village could sing anything. So, in admiration, the villagers called him Goopy Gyne—Goopy the Singer.

Although Goopy knew only that one song, he sang it quite often. He could not survive for long without singing it. If he did not sing, he felt he would suffocate. When he sang in his room, all the customers at his father's shop ran away. When he went to the field to sing, the cows broke their tethers and escaped. Finally, his father's customers stopped coming to the shop. The cowherds could no longer bring the cows to graze in the field. Kanu Kyne was so angry that he took a long bamboo stick and chased Goopy out of the house and to the field. In the field, the cowherds chased him, too, so Goopy ran to the forest and started doing his vocal warm-ups there.

There was another village close by. There lived a man called Paanchu Pyne. His son loved playing the drum. While he played the drum, he would go off in a trance, shake his legs, roll his eyes, bare his teeth and frown ferociously. The folks in his village would watch open-mouthed and exclaim: 'Aha! A-a-a-ah! O-Oh-oh Oh!' When the drummer would snarl like a tiger towards the end of his performance and say, 'Hah! Hah! Hah!' the villagers would not know where to run and just fall flat on the ground. The tiger-like growls and furious drumming earned him the name Bagha Byne—the Tiger Drummer, and he started being known by the name Bagha. Nobody remembered his real name any more.

Bagha would play the drum so hard that he would smash a drum everyday. Paanchu could no longer afford a new drum. But Bagha wanted to play his drum every day. The village-folk told Paanchu, 'If you can't afford it, we will collect money and pay for a new drum. We have such a maestro in our village, we can't have him stop playing his music.' So it was decided that the villagers would raise the money and buy Bagha a drum so strong that it would not break even with his vigorous drumming.

What a drum that was! The ends were three feet wide and the body was made of buffalo hide. Bagha was extremely pleased. He said, 'I will stand and play the drum.'

After that, he played the drum while standing, beating it with a pair of sticks. Even after playing it day and night, for one and a half months, he did not tear the skin of the drum. By then, his parents had gone crazy listening to his drumming, the villagers' heads were spinning. Who knows what would have happened if this would have continued for a few more days. But meanwhile the villagers came to Bagha, holding thick sticks in their hands and said, 'Dear Brother, we are giving you ten pots of delicious sweets; please go away somewhere else. Otherwise we will all go mad.'

What could Bagha do? He went to another village. But after two days the villagers there drove him out, too. Wherever he went, he was asked to leave. Everyday, he would wander in the fields and when hungry, he would go back to his own village and play the drums. The villagers would hurriedly give him a hearty meal, bid farewell and say, 'Phew! Saved!'

Soon things came to a pass and nobody offered to feed him anymore. As soon as the villagers heard his drum, they would chase him with sticks. Poor Bagha thought, 'There is no point staying with these idiots. It's better to go to the forest. The tiger may make a meal of me, but at least I can play my music.' He hauled the drum on his shoulders and went off to the forest.

Now Bagha was happy. Nobody chased him with sticks when he played the drum. There were no tigers or bears in the forest to eat him. There was only a Terrible Creature. Bagha had never seen it, only heard its call and trembled in fear, and thought, 'Dear Lord! If that creature comes here, it will swallow me along with my drum!'

That Terrible Creature was none other than Goopy Gyne. The wild calls that Bagha heard and trembled at were the sounds of Goopy warming up his voice. Goopy would also hear Bagha's drumming and tremble in fear, just like Bagha. Finally, he resolved, 'If I stay in this forest, I will die. I better escape from here.' Then he crept out of the forest. As soon as he stepped out of the trees he saw another man walking out of the forest with a huge drum on his head. Goopy asked him in surprise, 'Hey, who are you?'

Bagha said, 'I am Bagha Byne. Who are you?'

Goopy replied, 'I am Goopy Gyne. Where are you going?'

Bagha said, 'I am going wherever I get some shelter. The villagers are donkeys. They have no idea about good music. That's why I had escaped to the forest. But, Brother, I have heard the cries of a Terrible Creature in this forest. If I cross its path, I won't survive. That's why I am running away.'

Goopy asked, 'Really? I am also running after hearing a Terrible Creature's calls. Okay tell me, where did you hear the creature calling from?'

'From the eastern end of the forest. Below the banyan tree,' pointed Bagha.

Goopy exclaimed, 'Oh! That was me singing. Why should that be the cries of a Terrible Creature? This creature howls from the western end of the forest. From under the haritaki tree.'

Bagha laughed, 'But that is the sound of my drum! I was camping there.'

Now they understood that they had heard each other's music and had fled in fear. How they laughed! Then Goopy said, 'I am Gyne the Singer, you are Byne the Drummer. If we get together we can surely do something exciting.'

Bagha agreed with Goopy. They discussed plans and after several proposals they decided that they would go together and perform in front of the king. Surely, the king would be pleased to hear them. Maybe as a reward he would gift them half his kingdom or marry off his daughter to one of them.

Goopy and Bagha were now very happy with their plan to perform before the king. They laughed and danced their way to the banks of a big river. On the other side of the river was the king's palace.

There was a boat at the riverside to ferry them across. But the boatman wanted money. Goopy and Bagha had just arrived from the forest, where would they get any money from? They implored, 'Sir, we have no money. We can entertain you with our music instead. Please take us across.' The other passengers heard this and were very pleased. They told the boatman, 'We will collect money amongst us and pay their fare. Please take them along.'

The boatman had seen Bagha's drum and was eager to listen to the two musicians. So he did not fuss too much. Goopy and Bagha were allowed onboard and the boat set off.

The boat was crowded. There was no place to sit and perform. By the time Goopy and Bagha made space for themselves, the boat had reached mid-river. After humming a bit, Goopy started singing and Bagha struck the drum with his sticks. The boatful of passengers were startled by the sound of the music and rolled around, clutching each other in shock. And with that the boat overturned.

This was terribly dangerous. Thankfully, Bagha's drum was big enough for Goopy and him to cling onto for dear life. They did not reach the king's palace. Instead, they floated along the river all day and at dusk, they reached the bank of the river inside a dark and scary forest. This forest was frightening enough in the day; at night it was horrific. Bagha said, 'Brother Goopy, this is a scary place. What do we do?' Goopy said, 'What do you think? I will sing and you will play the drum. Since we will be eaten by tigers anyway, let us at least show them our talent.'

Bagha agreed heartily, 'You are right. We should die like maestros. Not like country bumpkins.'

Then, still in their wet clothes, the two of them started their music. Bagha's drum was wet too, because of which it produced a deep, somber sound. And Goopy was thinking that this was probably the last song of his life, so his voice was equally mournful. I can't tell you how grim that duet sounded. The music went on for hours. It was well past midnight but the two continued.

Suddenly, they felt that strange things were happening around them. Things that were hazy and black and huge seemed to be peeping from above the trees. These things had eyes like burning coal, and teeth like rows of shiny radish. Seeing them, Bagha's drumming stopped. The two friends' limbs curled up, their backs bent over, their necks sunk down, their eyes popped out and their mouths hung open. Their bodies started shaking and their teeth chattered so hard that they could not even make a run for it.

But the ghosts did not harm them. They were loving the music and wanted Goopy and Bagha to play at their king's son's wedding. When the music stopped, they chorused in their nasal voices, 'Why did you stop? Play, play, play.'

Goopy and Bagha felt encouraged on hearing this. They thought, 'This is fun. Let's sing and see what happens.'

As they resumed their music, the ghosts started climbing down from the trees in ones and twos and started dancing around them.

The scene cannot be described in words. Goopy and Bagha had never been appreciated by an audience like this. They danced and sang all night. As sunrise approached, the ghosts had to retreat. But before that they said, 'Come with us to our boss' son's wedding. We will make you happy.'

Goopy said, 'We want to go to the king's palace.' The ghosts said, 'You can go there later, first come and sing for us at the wedding. We will reward you.'

So they went to the ghosts' dwelling. It's difficult to describe the music that they performed at the wedding. But as they bade farewell, the ghosts asked, 'What do you wish for?'

Goopy replied, 'We want to please people with our music.' The ghosts said, 'Very well. When you perform, your audience will be frozen in their places till you end your performance. What else do you wish for?'

Goopy said, 'We want to be well-fed and well-clothed at all times.'

The ghosts gave them a bag and said, 'When you put your hands inside this bag, you will get whatever you want to eat or wear. What else do you want?'

Goopy said, 'I can't think of anything more to ask for.' Then the ghosts burst out laughing and handed them two pairs of shoes and said, 'When you wear these shoes and wish to go to any place, you will immediately be transported there.'

Now they had no worries. Goopy and Bagha said goodbye to the ghosts, wore the shoes and said, 'We want to go to the king's palace.' Immediately the forest disappeared and they found themselves standing in front of the gate of a huge house. They had never seen such a big and beautiful house. They immediately understood that this was the king's palace.

But now there was a big problem. At the gate of the

palace stood a few ugly and ferocious-looking gatekeepers. When they saw Goopy and Bagha approaching the gate with their large drum, they snarled at them rudely, 'Hey you two! Where do you think you are going?'

Goopy stammered, 'Sir, we have come to perform for His Majesty.' This irritated the guards even more. They waved their sticks at them and shouted, 'Get lost from here!'

Goopy was not to be discouraged by a few ugly guards. He snorted, 'Eesh! We will surely go to the king.' As soon as he uttered these words, the magic shoes transported them to the king's room.

The king was sleeping in his bedroom, his queen was sitting near his head and gently fanning him. Suddenly, out of nowhere and with no warning, Goopy and Bagha arrived in the room with their drum.

The ghostly shoes had magic that allowed them to go past closed doors and windows, and impenetrable walls. But the sudden appearance of the two musicians startled everyone. The queen screamed in fear and fainted right there. The king jumped up and stated running around like a lunatic. There was chaos all over the palace. All the guards and sentries came rushing, brandishing their swords and shields.

In the hullabaloo, Goopy and Bagha got equally confused. They could have just commanded their shoes to take them out of there. But they had completely forgotten about that. Instead they tried to run. That did not take them too far—two steps later they were caught and spanked hard by the guards. Shoes, sticks, whips, punches, slaps, ear-twisting—they got it all. Finally, the king ordered, 'Throw these two into the jail. Keep them there for three days. After that I will decide whether their heads are to be chopped off or they are to be fed to the dogs.'

Poor Goopy! Poor Bagha! They had come to the king, hoping to be rewarded for their music. Instead what a mess they had landed in! They were tied in ropes by the guards and thrown into a dark cell. Sitting there, the first day, they could barely move. Their bodies were aching from the beating they had got. But far more disastrous was the loss of Bagha's drum. Bagha thumped his chest and wailed loudly, 'Oh Goopy! Oh, oh, awwww! Oh, Goopy! I don't repent that I was beaten! Or even if I die! But I lost my drum!'

By then Goopy had calmed down. He patted Bagha and said, 'Don't fear. So what if you lost the drum? We still have the shoes and the bag. We are very stupid. That's why we got beaten up. Anyway, let bygones be bygones, now let's have some fun.'

Bagha calmed down, 'What fun shall we have?'

Goopy said, 'First let's have the fun of eating. Then we will think of other fun things to do.'

Then he put his hand into the magic bag and said, 'Come on now, give us a pot of pulao.' At once, a wonderful fragrance filled the air! Even kings did not have such delicious pulao everyday. And it was a huge pot! Goopy struggled to lift the pot out of the bag.

Somehow he dragged it out and then ordered more food, 'Fries, vegetable korma, chutney, sweets, yoghurt, pudding, sherbet—bring quickly!' Soon the room was filled with delicious dishes served on dinner plates made of gold and silver. How much could the two of them eat? After eating to their heart's content, all the aches and pains disappeared.

Then Bagha said, 'Brother, let us escape now. Otherwise they will feed us to the dogs.' Goopy said, 'Are you crazy? How will they feed us to the dogs when we have our magical footwear? Let's wait and see what happens next.' Bagha was mighty pleased to hear this. He knew that Goopy would play some pranks.

Two days went by. The next morning the king was going to give his decision on the fate of the musicians. That night, Goopy put his hand inside the bag and said, 'We want royal clothes.' Immediately, there emerged from the bag clothes that were so beautiful that they could not have been stitched by mortals. Goopy and Bagha wore these clothes, placed their old clothes and the utensils in a sack, slipped on their magical shoes and announced, 'Now we will go to the fields to get some fresh air.' They were immediately taken to the large field next to the palace. They hid the sack of clothes in a corner of the field and strolled up to the palace.

The palace guards had seen them walking towards the gate and had run off and announced to the king, 'Your Majesty, two kings have arrived at the palace.' The king came to the gate to welcome them in. A splendid room was opened up for them. Many servants, cooks and guards were sent to look after them.

Goopy and Bagha washed their hands and feet and had some refreshing snacks. After that, the king came to meet them. Seeing their grand costumes he wondered, 'They must be kings of large kingdoms.' He asked Goopy, 'Which kingdoms do you rule?' Goopy joined his palms humbly and replied, 'Your Highness! How can we be kings? We are your servants.'

Although Goopy was speaking the truth, the king did not believe him. He thought, 'What humble people! And so soft spoken! They are great kings and also gentlemen.' He did not say anything further and took them to his royal court. The king was to pass his judgement on the two miscreants who had broken into his bedroom three days ago. The time for the judgment was upon them, and the guards went to fetch the criminals. But would they find them? When their room that had been locked for three days was unlocked, the guards discovered that it was empty.

Then there was a lot of shouting and running around. The chief of guards was very angry and started scolding his men. The hapless guards begged for mercy, 'Sir, it's not our fault. We locked them in and stood outside the doors for three days. Those two were not humans. They were ghosts. How else could they have escaped from that room?'

Everyone was convinced by this argument. The king, who was so angry and had ordered the chief to be beheaded, changed his stance, 'Yes, I am certain that those two were ghosts. My room was also shut. How did they enter it with their huge drum?'

Then everyone agreed, 'Yes, yes, correct, those two are ghosts.' As they said this, they shuddered, sweat trickling down their bodies. Then they remembered Bagha's drum and said, 'Your Highness! Ghostly drums are very dangerous. Don't keep it in your room. Burn the drum.'

The king agreed, 'Good Lord! A ghost's drum in my room! Bring it right away and burn it.'

That day, Goopy had such a trying time with Bagha! Bagha had started crying at the mention of his drum being burnt. God knows what he would do if they actually burnt it. He would hardly be able to keep it a secret that the drum was his. Goodness! Now they were sure to get caught and be executed.

Goopy was very tempted to take Bagha and flee from there. But that was not possible. When they sat in the court, they had taken off their ghostly shoes.

Meanwhile, the court saw Bagha wailing and chaos ensued amongst the people. Everyone thought that he had some grave illness and that he would die soon. The royal doctor arrived and checked his pulse and nodded somberly in despair. He prescribed a laxative medicine and applied a poultice of herbs on his tummy. The doctor said, 'If his pain does not heal with this treatment then we have to apply poultice on his back and then on his two sides.'

Hearing this awful prescription, Bagha stopped

wailing. The people thought his pain had disappeared with the doctor's miracle medicines.

Anyway, Bagha saw that his crying had diverted attention from the proposal to burn his drum. So despite the painful poultice on his tummy, he calmed down. The king escorted him with care to his room and helped him to lie down. Goopy sat next to him and fanned him.

When everyone had left the room, Goopy said, 'Shame, brother! You should not cry like this, just anywhere. See what a lot of trouble we got into.' Bagha said, 'If I wouldn't have cried they would have burnt my drum. I am having to bear the painful poultice but at least my drum is safe.'

While Goopy and Bagha were chatting, the chief of guards had returned to the royal court and whispered to the king, 'Your Highness, please grant me permission to speak.'

The king replied, 'What is it?'

The chief said, 'Your Highness, that man who was rolling around and crying, and his friend are those two ghosts. I recognized them.' The king said, 'You are right, my chap, I, too, had this same suspicion. This is a big problem. What do we do now?'

Then all the courtiers started whispering. Some said, 'Call an exorcist to remove them.' Others said, 'If the exorcist is not able to remove them then they may get angry and destroy us. It's better to burn them when they are asleep.'

Everybody liked the idea but the problem was that if

they tried to burn the ghosts, the palace would also be burnt down with them. After a lot of discussion, it was decided that the ghosts would be moved to a garden-house. If the garden-house burnt down, it wouldn't be a big loss. The king said, 'Take the drum to the garden-house too. If it burns along with the garden-house, all our problems will be solved.'

Goopy and Bagha were very happy to hear of the plan to move them to the garden-house. Of course, they had no idea that there was a devious conspiracy behind it. They thought that the quiet garden-house would allow them to practice their music at peace. The area was very pretty. The house was made of wood and was very beautiful. Bagha recovered as soon as they moved there. Goopy told him, 'What is the purpose of staying on over here? Come, let us leave.' But Bagha said, 'This is such a pretty place, let us stay for a couple of days more. Aha, I wish I had my drum!'

Later that day, Bagha was wandering in the rooms of the house and Goopy was sitting in a corner of the garden and humming a tune. Suddenly, Bagha started yelling loudly. Goopy could not decipher what Bagha was shouting, except loud yells of, 'Goopy! Goopy!' He ran in and saw that Bagha was prancing around the house with his drum on his head. He was so excited to find the drum in the room that he could barely speak. After half an hour of dancing in joy, Bagha calmed down and said, 'See, my drum was in this room. Oh! I'm so excited! Hahaha!' And he danced for another ten minutes. Then he said, 'After such a lot of trouble I have got the drum back. Please sing a song and I will play the drum.' Goopy replied, 'Not now, I'm very hungry. Let us eat. After dinner, we can sit in the verandah and sing.'

But the king had decided that they would burn the house and the musicians with it that night. The chief of guards had been ordered to arrange for a banquet in the evening, at the garden-house. The chief would be present at the feast with fifty–sixty people. After the meal, when Goopy and Bagha went to bed, they would set fire all around the house and close all ways to escape.

They all had a hearty meal. Goopy and Bagha had planned to start playing their music as soon as the guests left. But the chief was waiting anxiously for them to sleep! When it was obvious that he wouldn't leave till they had slept, Goopy took Bagha to the bedroom and they started snoring loudly.

After sometime, when Goopy and Bagha saw that everyone had left and silence had fallen over the house, they went to the verandah and started playing the drum and singing.

Meanwhile, the chief had ordered his troops: 'Set fire properly to every door. And don't leave till the fire is burning properly.' He went to set fire on the staircase himself and was planning to run once it was burning merrily. Just at that time, Bagha's drumbeats and Goopy's singing started. Then it was impossible for the chief or any of his troops to move from their positions. They were all burnt to death. Seeing the fire, Goopy and Bagha wore their shoes, picked up their magic bag and the drum and escaped.

The chief died in the fire but a few people survived. These survivors went to the king and related their experience to him. The king was spooked. The next day, a few more people arrived at the court and said that they had gone to watch the fire burn. There they heard some strange music and had seen the two ghosts fly off and disappear. Hearing this, the king started trembling in fear. He cancelled his court for that day and returned to his palace. He shut his bedroom door tight, for the fear of ghosts, hid under a thick blanket and lay there trembling. He did not leave the room for a month.

In the meantime, Goopy and Bagha escaped from the fire and reached the forest near their villages, where they had first met. They decided to meet their parents after all these adventures. As soon as they reached the forest, Bagha said, 'Goopy, isn't this where we had met?' Goopy nodded, 'Yes.' Bagha said, 'How can we leave this place without playing some music?' Goopy agreed, 'You are right! Let's start.' And then they started singing and playing heartily.

Now, a very strange incident had happened. A band of dacoits had stolen from the treasury of the King of Halla and also kidnapped his two little sons. The king gave chase with his soldiers but could not catch them. As Goopy and Bagha started their loud music, the dacoits were passing through the forest. But once the music started, the dacoits could not move. The music continued through the night and the dacoits had to stand in the forest. Early in the morning, the King of Halla arrived and arrested the whole group. When he heard that he was able to catch the dacoits because of Goopy and Bagha's music, he was full of joy and showered them with affection. The two little princes told the king, 'Father, you would never have heard such fantastic music. Let's take them with us.' The king told Goopy and Bagha, 'Come along with me. I will pay you five hundred rupees as your monthly salary.'

Hearing this, Goopy joined his palms and saluting the king, he said, 'Your Majesty, please grant us leave for two days. We want to visit our parents and after taking their permission we will reach your capital city.' The king said, 'Okay, we will rest in this forest for two days. Go and see your parents and come back here.'

Goopy's parents had been very sad after he had left. They were overjoyed to see him return home. But Bagha had no such luck. His parents had died a few days back. The villagers saw him coming with his drum and said, 'Look! This fellow will again trouble us with his music. Beat him up!' Bagha pleaded, 'I have only come to see my parents. I will stay for two days. I won't play my drum.' But nobody listened to him. They snarled at him, told him that his parents were dead and chased him with sticks. Bagha ran for his life and threw bricks at the villagers, breaking their legs. Blood flowed from the heads and the legs of the injured villagers.

Goopy was sitting in his front yard and talking to his

father when he saw Bagha limping and running towards his house. His clothes were torn and covered in blood. He rushed to Bagha and asked, 'What happened? Why are you in this state?' Bagha's face broke into smiles on seeing Goopy. Panting hard, he said, 'I barely survived! Those idiots would have broken my drum.'

In Goopy's house, Bagha was looked after by Goopy and his parents and he recovered. After two days, they told his parents, 'Goodbye. Be ready. We will come back soon and take you with us.'

A few months went by. Goopy and Bagha were happily settled in the palace of the King of Halla. They had become famous all over the world. Whoever heard them said, 'There haven't been such music maestros in the past, and there won't be in the future!' The king loved them a lot. He could not survive a day without hearing their music. He would tell Goopy all about his life, the good and the bad. One day, Goopy noticed that the king looked forlorn. He seemed to be very thoughtful, as though anticipating a disaster. Finally, he told Goopy, 'I am in great trouble. God knows what will happen. The King of Shundi is coming to attack my kingdom.'

Now, the King of Shundi was the same king who had tried to kill Goopy and Bagha in the terrible fire. As soon as he heard the name of the King of Shundi, Goopy had a brilliant idea. He told the King of Halla, 'Your Majesty, do not worry. Order this servant of yours and I will make this into a comedy of errors.' The king smiled wanly and said, 'Goopy, you are a musician. You have no idea about wars. The King of Shundi has a strong and large army. How will I defeat them?' Goopy said, 'If you give me permission, I can try. It won't cause any harm.' The king said, 'Okay, you do what you wish.' Goopy was very pleased and called Bagha to discuss his plan.

That day, Goopy and Bagha planned for a long time. Bagha was very excited! He said, 'We will do something together. But I am scared of one thing. If we suddenly need to run, I may forget about our shoes and start running like a regular person and will get beaten up. That's how I got beaten up by those village idiots.'

Goopy reassured Bagha that this won't happen again. Next day, they started rolling out their plan. Every night they would go to Shundi and wander around the palace gathering local news. The battle plans being made in Shundi seemed frightening. If they attacked Halla with this plan then there was no saving the kingdom of Halla. Prayers were being held in the palace-temple. The king would leave for Halla with his army after pleasing the gods with his prayers.

Goopy and Bagha saw the preparations and locked themselves in their room. They put their hands in the magic bag and said, 'We want some new and delicious sweets.' At this command, the sweets that came out of the bag were indescribable. Nobody had seen or eaten such sweets before. Goopy and Bagha took these delectable sweets and went and sat in the tower of the temple. Below them, the prayer ceremonies were going on in full swing. The temple courtyard was filled with people, the fragrance of incense sticks, the sound of conch shells and the chatter of people talking. Goopy and Bagha dropped the bag of sweets into the crowd from their perch on the temple tower and watched the fun. In the dark and amidst the smoke from the incense sticks, nobody could see them sitting there.

There was silence when the sweets landed in the yard. Several people jumped in surprise and some screamed and ran away. A few brave people picked up some sweets and looked at them closely under the lights of the lamps. Then one of them closed his eyes and popped the sweet into his mouth. The taste left him speechless. After that he kept picking sweets from the floor, putting them into his mouth, dancing and shouting in delight. Suddenly the whole courtyard was full of people scrambling to eat the sweets and snatching them from each other's hands.

Some people rushed to the king and announced, 'Your Majesty, the gods are so happy with our prayers that they have sent divine sweets from heaven. The sweets are so tasty!' As soon as the king heard that, he hurriedly ran towards the temple, tucking the pleats of his ceremonial loincloth.

But alas, by then all the sweets were over. The courtyard was swept for some crumbs for the king but nothing was found. The king was very annoyed. 'This is so unfair! I do the prayers and all of you eat the divine sweets. Not a crumb left for me! I will behead all of you!' The people trembled in fear and begged, 'Please, Your Highness! We didn't finish the sweets. They disappeared suddenly after we had eaten some. Please forgive us today. Tomorrow we will keep all sweets for you, Sire.' The king said, 'Alright, remember that! Don't you dare eat any sweets tomorrow.'

Next day, the king came to the temple in the morning and waited, staring at the sky, praying that the sweets would fall. The rest of the crowd sat at a distance, watching the fun. The prayers were going on with even greater pomp. Everyone was thinking that today the gods will send sweets for the king which would be even more delicious.

Later that night, Goopy and Bagha got a variety of new and delectable sweets from their magical bag and sat on the temple tower. They were wearing glamorous dresses, crowns on their heads, necklaces around their necks, bracelets on their wrists and earrings on their ears. They were dressed like the gods. Nothing was visible through the smoke but the king was sitting and staring at the sky. Suddenly, Goopy and Bagha laughed out aloud and dropped the sweets on the king's head. He screamed and jumped three feet into the air. Then, he recovered and started stuffing his mouth with sweets, with both hands, while dancing a merry jig at the same time.

While this was going on, Goopy and Bagha came down from the top of the temple and stood in front of the King of Shundi. 'The gods have come!' everybody shouted and started prostrating themselves on the floor as a mark of respect. The king just lay flat on the ground in front of them and kept striking his head on the ground. Goopy said kindly, 'Your Majesty, we enjoyed your dance a lot. Come, let us embrace.' The king was overwhelmed. How many people had the good fortune to be embraced by the gods?

They started embracing. The crowds yelled, 'Victory! Victory!' Goopy and Bagha took this opportunity and grabbed the king from both sides. They said in a loud voice, 'Now we will go to our room.' Immediately, the three of them were transported to their room. The crowds at the temple stood staring at the sky with their mouths open for a long time. When the king did not return, they went back to their homes and said, 'What a miracle we witnessed! The king ascended to heaven in his human form! The gods came themselves to take him away.'

By then, the king had fainted in Goopy and Bagha's laps. He remained unconscious for a while even after reaching their room. At dawn, when he opened his eyes, he saw that the two ghosts were sitting near his head. He fell at their feet at once and trembled and begged, 'Sirs! Please don't eat me! I will sacrifice two hundred buffaloes in your names and pray for mercy.'

Goopy said, 'Your Highness, don't be afraid. We are not ghosts and we won't eat you.' The king was not convinced; he did not utter another word, just held his head in his hands and sat and shook in fear.

After that, Bagha went to the King of Halla and said, 'Last night we captured the King of Shundi. What is your command now?'

The King of Halla said, 'Bring him here.'

When the two kings met, the King of Shundi

understood that he had been captured. He realized that he would not be able to conquer Halla and maybe he would be killed. But the King of Halla did not kill him, just took his crown and kingdom away.

Then he told Goopy and Bagha, 'You have saved us. Otherwise I would have lost my country and my life. I am giving you half the kingdom of Shundi to rule and my two daughters in marriage to both of you.'

After that there were celebrations galore. Goopy and Bagha became the sons-in-law of the King of Halla and ruled Shundi while practising their wonderful music. Honour and contentment filled the lives of Goopy's parents.

notes on authors

Edward Lear (1812–1888) was an artist, illustrator, musician, author and poet, now known mostly for his nonsense poetry, prose and especially his limericks. His nonsense collections of poems, songs, and short stories are still popular. He also made botanical drawings and wrote recipes.

Mary de Morgan (1850–1907) was the author of three volumes of fairy tales. Her works deviate from the fairy tale norm by often not including a happy ending, or not having the protagonist gain wealth or power. Instead they gain the wisdom of recognizing the value of living without these things.

H.G. Wells (1866–1946) wrote dozens of novels, short stories and works of social commentary, history, satire, biography, and autobiography. He is best remembered for his science fiction novels. His most notable science fiction works include *The Time Machine* (1895), *The Invisible Man* (1897) and *The War of the Worlds* (1898).

Charles Dickens (1812–1870) created some of the world's best-known fictional characters and is regarded by many as the greatest novelist of the Victorian era. His works enjoyed unprecedented popularity during his lifetime, and his novels and short stories are still widely read today.

Lewis Carroll or Charles Lutwidge Dodgson (1832–1898) was the writer of children's fiction like *Alice's Adventures in Wonderland* and its sequel *Through the Looking-Glass*. He wrote the classic nonsense poems *Jabberwocky* and *The Hunting of the Snark*. He was also a mathematician and a photographer.

L. Frank Baum (1856–1919) was an American author chiefly famous for his children's books, particularly *The Wonderful Wizard of Oz* and its sequels. He wrote fourteen novels in the *Oz* series, besides numerous other novels, short stories and poems. The 1939 adaptation of the first *Oz* book would become a landmark of 20th-century cinema.

Edith Nesbit (1858–1924) was an author and poet. She published her books for children under the name of E. Nesbit. She wrote or collaborated on more than sixty books for children. Among her best-known books are *The Story of the Treasure Seekers* and *The Railway Children*.

Upendrakishore Ray Chowdhury (1863–1915) was a prolific children's writer from Bengal. His works *Goopy Gyne Bagha Byne*, *Tuntunir Boi*, *Chheleder Ramayan*, *Chheleder Mahabharat* and more, are all classics of Bengali children's literature. He edited and published the children's magazine *Sandesh*, for which he wrote and illustrated stories, poems and essays. He was also a pioneering printer, musician, entrepreneur and painter.

Tilottama Shome is an architect by training and wanderer by profession. Her early childhood days were spent in Calcutta when most of her time went in reading children's fiction, both in Bengali and English. Nowadays, she lives in Delhi with her family. She has translated *The Children's Ramayana* by Upendrakishore Ray Chowdhury.

ALSO IN TALKING CUB CLASSICS

A CHRISTMAS CAROL AND OTHER CHRISTMAS STORIES

CHARLES DICKENS
Introduction by Gillian Wright

Curl up and sink into this classic, much-loved story about an old man, three ghosts, and the much-needed Christmas spirit.

Ebenezer Scrooge is a mean, grumpy, joyless old man. He does not believe in being generous or happy, even at Christmas time. All he wants to do is to sit in his dingy office and count his money. But one Christmas Eve, he goes home to bed and is visited by the ghost of his dead partner, Marley, who warns Scrooge that he will soon be visited by three more ghosts. And indeed, they appear: the Ghosts of Christmas Past, Present and Future. They show Scrooge three visions that make him think about all that he has done wrong in his life and how he could have made it different.

A Christmas Carol has been immortalised in in print, films and plays for over a century. In this edition, it is accompanied by some of Charles Dickens' famous Christmas short stories that are just as heart-warming and supremely enjoyable.

Timeless, inspirational, humorous, and with a delightful introduction by Gillian Wright, this book is a Christmas gift to be read and loved on any day of the year.

ALSO IN TALKING CUB CLASSICS

THE JUNGLE BOOK STORIES

RUDYARD KIPLING

Introduction by Ranjit Lal

From the icy Arctic to the forests of India, meet all kinds of animals in this classic collection of stories from the Jungle Book

Kotick is an unusual seal. Not only is his fur white, but he is also filled with curiosity and a sense of adventure. After he witnesses the brutal killing of seals by humans, he decides to find a place where no human can reach. And so begins his search through the icy waters of the Arctic. Can he find such a place and claim the leadership of his pack of seals? Rikki-Tikki-Tavi is a clever mongoose who is determined to protect the human family he lives with. What happens when Nag, the cobra, shows up in the garden with evil plans on his mind? Mugger of Mugger-Ghaut has lived an exciting life and tells grand stories to Jackal and Adjutant Crane, little knowing that the greatest threat is lurking close by in the form of the White Man.

Elephants who dance, camels that talk, tailor birds with louder voices than brains, the desolation of an Arctic winter, high tales of cunning and bravery—all of these come alive in the brilliance of Rudyard Kipling's writing. Go wild with this collection of stories on and about animals from the classic *Jungle Book*, now with a wonderful introduction by Ranjit Lal.

www.ingramcontent.com/pod-product-compliance
Lightning Source LLC
LaVergne TN
LVHW021822060526
838201LV00058B/3483